"I'M THE DEMON."

Ariel's jeans were in flames. She almost laughed. This was cool. Just as she was beginning to enjoy herself, a shadow tackled her and smothered her, forcing her to roll in the spiky grass. The hot, liquid tingle vanished.

"Hey!" Ariel protested.

She sat up straight. Leslie was right beside her. She looked awful. Her face was smeared with black stains. Her hair was a mess. Her lungs were heaving.

"What's going on?" Ariel muttered. "What are you—"

"Take your pants off," Leslie gasped.

Ariel blinked. "Uh . . . what?"

"*Do* it!"

Ariel glanced down at her legs again. The fire was out. Her jeans were black and shredded. A foul-smelling steam rose from the fabric. Holding her breath, she bent down and rolled up the cuff.

"My God," she whispered.

The material was still very hot, but the flesh underneath was unscathed.

It wasn't even *red*. It was the same unblemished white it had always been. She felt sick. "Look at me. Nothing happened. Nothing—"

"It's okay," Leslie soothed, gently wrapping her arms around Ariel's shoulders. "Don't worry about it. We'll figure it out."

A tear fell from Ariel's cheek. She shook her head. "What's there to figure out? I'm the Demon. I can't get hurt."

About the Author

Daniel Parker is the author of over twenty books for children and young adults. He lives in New York City with his wife, a dog, and a psychotic cat named Bootsie. He is a Leo. When he isn't writing, he is tirelessly traveling the world on a doomed mission to achieve rock-and-roll stardom. As of this date, his musical credits include the composition of bluegrass sound-track numbers for the film *The Grave* (starring a bloated Anthony Michael Hall) and a brief stint performing live rap music to baffled Filipino audiences in Hong Kong. Mr. Parker once worked in a cheese shop. He was fired.

COUNT DOWN

SEPTEMBER

by
Daniel Parker

Simon & Schuster

First Aladdin Paperbacks edition August 1999

Copyright © 1999 by 17th Street Productions,
a division of Daniel Weiss Associates, Inc.
and Daniel Ehrenhaft
Cover art copyright © 1999 by 17th Street Productions,
a division of Daniel Weiss Associates, Inc.

 Produced by 17th Street Productions,
a division of Daniel Weiss Associates, Inc.
33 West 17th Street, New York, NY 10011

Cover design by Mike Rivilis

Aladdin Paperbacks
An imprint of Simon & Schuster
Children's Publishing Division
1230 Avenue of the Americas
New York, NY 10020

ISBN: 978-1-4814-2594-0

To Mike Sullivan

SEPTEMBER

The Ancient Scroll
of the Scribes:

In the ninth lunar cycles.
During the last of 5759 and
the first of 5760.
The Demon and the Chosen One
will draw close.
And the Demon will latch
on to the Chosen One.
Following her incessantly.
filling her head with lies,
Spreading deceit about the Seers.
Weaving magic to draw
attention away from herself.
Even as the Chosen One's true
followers are led astray.
Those who follow the False Prophet will be
dispersed on orders from the Demon's servants.
Spreading in all directions to draw
the believers to a place of fiery death.
And the Demon shall steal the key
to the Future Time from the Chosen One.

A shovel can help change news.
Cut the pie and save it.
Run for the choice to cry.
Stone a clock to miss delays.
Nine nine ninety-nine.

The countdown has started . . .

The long sleep is over.

For three thousand years I have patiently watched and waited. The Prophecies foretold the day when the sun would reach out and touch the earth—when my slumber would end, when my ancient weapon would breathe, when my dormant glory would blaze once more upon the planet and its people.

That day has arrived.

But there can be no triumph without a battle. Every civilization tells the same story. Good requires evil; redemption requires sin. The legends are as varied as are the civilizations that spawned them— yet each contains that same nugget of truth.

So I am not alone. The Chosen One awaits me. The flare opened the inner eyes of the Visionaries, those who can join the Chosen One to prevent my reign. But in order for them to defeat me, they must first make sense of their visions.

For you see, every vision is a piece of a puzzle, a puzzle that will eventually form a picture . . . a picture that I will shatter into a billion pieces and reshape in the image of my choosing.

I am prepared. My servants knew of this day. They made the necessary preparations to confuse the Visionaries—all in anticipation of that glorious time when the countdown ends and my ancient weapon ushers in the New Era.

My servants unleashed the plague that reduced the earth's population to a scattered horde of frightened adolescents. None of these children know how or why their elders and youngers perished.

And that was only the beginning.

My servants have descended upon the chaos. They will subvert the Prophecies in order to convert the masses into unknowing slaves. They will hunt down the Visionaries, one by one, until all are dead. They will eliminate the descendants of the Scribes so that none of the Visionaries will learn of the scroll. The hidden codes shall remain hidden. Terrible calamities and natural disasters will wreak havoc upon the earth. Even the Chosen One will be helpless against me.

I *will* triumph.

sePARTember

September 1, 1999

Puget Drive,
Babylon, Washington
9:35 A.M.

"We have to find her!"

"No. That's exactly what Ariel wants. She wants us to follow—"

"How do *you* know? You don't have visions. . . ."

It's never going to end, Sarah Levy thought. She'd been sprawled on the lawn of an abandoned suburban house all night, bombarded by the same scraps of frightened conversation. Nothing had been solved. No decisions had been made. Nobody had even slept. The sun was already high in the sky, warming the gentle ocean breeze that swept through the pine trees . . . but the mob of kids kept arguing, milling from one dying bonfire to the next. The scene reminded her of the way Tel Aviv used to be after a clash between Palestinians and Israelis: There was the same electric tension in the street—as if everyone expected violence to erupt again without warning.

We've all witnessed something terrible.

Even now Sarah still couldn't quite believe that she had actually looked the Demon in the eye. Of course, she hadn't really concentrated on Lilith's

5

face . . . or Ariel, or whatever the Demon's name was. No, Sarah's horrified gaze had been drawn to something else: the bloody, open gash in Ariel's chest—the fatal wound that should have killed her but didn't.

She can't be destroyed, Sarah realized. *She can't be stopped. They plunged a knife into her heart, and nothing happened. She's just like my granduncle's scroll. Indestructible. She uses the same kind of magic.*

But even as fear crept over Sarah, she felt something else—a flicker of hope. If the Demon couldn't be killed, maybe Sarah couldn't be killed, either. Sarah was the Chosen One, after all. She was the Demon's nemesis. She might be blessed with those powers too, the same powers as the Demon and the ancient Hebrew parchment lying in the weeds at her side—

"I can't find her anywhere."

Sarah squinted up into the sunlight. George Porter slumped down beside her, shaking his head. He sniffed loudly and wiped his nose on the sleeve of his grubby leather jacket. His jaw was tight. His piercing green eyes seemed clouded, distant.

"I looked all over the place," he added, brushing his blond bangs out of his face.

"What did you expect?" Sarah asked. "She's probably hundreds of miles away by now."

"No, no," he said. "Not the Demon. I know *she's* gone. She stole our freaking car, remember? I'm talking about Julia. She doesn't even know I'm *alive*. She thinks I died back at Harold's farm. I have to track her down."

Whoops. Sarah swallowed, unsure of what to say. In all the chaos and confusion, she'd forgotten about George's missing girlfriend—and his obsession with finding her.

"I'm sorry," she finally mumbled.

"Me too." His eyes wandered over to the scroll, half hidden by the tall grass. "Maybe the prophecies can help. I mean, we know Julia's with that bastard Harold. He's the False Prophet, right? Does it say where the False Prophet is?"

Sarah hesitated. George's gruff, streetwise manner still caught her off guard. For somebody who truly believed that she was the Chosen One, he was just so . . . *harsh*. But then she supposed it was natural, given where he came from. She'd never really known anyone like him—a delinquent from a broken home, a petty criminal with no family or education. Yet he was also sensitive and considerate and utterly devoted to his girlfriend. He was like two people wrapped in one.

"I don't think so," she said after a moment. "I could take another look. . . ." But she knew it wouldn't help. She'd been studying the scroll all night, searching for clues about how to defeat the Demon. All she found were vague, mysterious descriptions of how she and the Demon were supposed to "draw close." It didn't make any sense. The Demon wasn't even in town anymore. And there was only one line about the False Prophet— something about how his followers were going to disperse on orders from the Demon's servants. What did *that* mean?

"How about that secret code thing?" George pressed. "Any luck cracking it?"

Sarah glanced at him, then lowered her head. "No," she admitted. "I mean, I'm getting closer. I know it has something to do with the way I translate those bits of nonsense I was telling you about—at least, I *think* it does." She looked up at him. "Actually, I'm more confused than ever. I thought the Demon's name was Lilith, not Ariel. And are you *sure* this is where we're supposed to be? In this town?"

"I'm sure," George said grimly. "It was like I was dragged here. You saw how bad it was. And that cliff down the street . . . it's the one I saw in my visions. I know it." He waved his hands around at the disheveled teenagers. "Besides, why else would all these Visionaries be hanging out in the same place? *Something's* gonna happen. Believe me." He took a deep breath. "That's why Julia should be here. I don't get it."

I know what you mean, Sarah thought. She didn't get it, either. When she peered down the tree-lined street at the rows of identical split-level homes, she just couldn't bring herself to accept that *this* was the spot. In a strange way, she was almost disappointed. Why would an ultimate, apocalyptic confrontation take place *here?* She had envisioned a snowy mountaintop or a scorched desert wasteland—some kind of profoundly dramatic landscape. Not suburbia. With all the smoldering bonfires, the whole atmosphere smacked of a block party gone stale.

I've traveled halfway around the world for this.

She shook her head. Why was the Demon waiting for her in Washington? The scroll had been written three thousand years ago. In Hebrew. In Israel. Sarah had found it in Jerusalem. Shouldn't the Demon be waiting *there?* Didn't the Bible say that the Final Days would start in Jerusalem? Her brother, Josh, would know, if he were still alive.

"It's so weird," she said after a long while. "I mean, if this is the place, then why did the Demon run off? There's nothing in the scroll about it."

George shrugged. "Maybe she's gonna come back. Or maybe you gotta do something to *make* her come back."

Sarah frowned. "What do you mean?"

"You still haven't taken charge," he answered simply. "Look at these kids. All of them came here to find the Chosen One, and you still haven't told them who you really are. What are you waiting for?"

"I . . . I . . . ," she started, but she couldn't finish. The truth was that she had no idea what to do. She always faced the same old dilemma: How could she *prove* who she was? Why was it so difficult? There was never a bolt of lightning, or an earthquake, or some kind of cataclysmic event that stated: *Here is the Chosen One!* No. She'd always had to rely on her wits or a miraculous stroke of luck. She could never seem to plan anything. Even

9

the scroll's prophecies didn't help. They only seemed to make sense in hindsight.

"If I were you, I'd go over to one of those fires and toss in the scroll," George muttered. "Or rip it into shreds and show the Visionaries how it fixes itself. You just gotta make 'em believe. It's not hard. I didn't believe you at first, either, remember? Step up and show 'em your magic. You know what I'm saying?"

Sarah absently fiddled with her glasses, pushing them up on the bridge of her nose. Maybe George was right. It was time to stop being so passive. Maybe she should take matters into her own hands for once instead of just waiting.

"What *does* the scroll say about this month, anyway?" George asked.

"Not a whole lot I can understand." She shook her head. "It says that the Demon's going to follow me around and fill my head with lies. It also says that she's going to steal 'the key to the Future Time'—whatever that means."

George snorted. "Maybe it means our car."

"Yeah, right." She managed a tired laugh. It *was* pretty odd that Ariel had stolen that beat-up blue Chevy. Ariel had displayed the most awesome magic—the power of immortality. Why hadn't she just disappeared in a puff of black smoke? Why did she have to resort to something as banal as auto theft?

"So the Demon has *gotta* come back," George said. "She can't follow you around if she's not here."

Sarah nodded. "You know, you're right." She stood and stretched, then stooped to gather up the worn rolls of parchment. If she stayed put, the Demon would find her; it was written in the Prophecies. It *had* to happen. She tucked the scroll under her arm and surveyed the crowded street. It was time to "take charge," as George had advised. These Visionaries were scared. They needed reassurance. They needed to know that she was finally here. . . .

"So how do you think I should do this?" she asked.

But George didn't answer. He was already scrambling out to the street and cupping his hands around his mouth.

"George?" Sarah called. "What—"

"Hey, everybody!" he shouted. "Listen up! Come here! Check this out!"

Check what out? she wondered angrily. *What is he doing?*

A few heads turned.

"The Chosen One is here!" George cried. He flung an outstretched arm back at Sarah. "She's gonna tell you about the Demon!"

Oh, no. How could he do this? She needed to *think* first, to figure something out—

"She's got a magic scroll that's filled with all kinds of prophecies! It talks about our visions. She'll tell us what they mean!"

What they mean? Sarah felt her cheeks grow warm. George was *not* being smart. No, he was being very stupid. How could she tell people what the prophecies meant if *she* didn't know herself?

11

The street suddenly grew very quiet.

George turned to her. "Go on," he urged.

Sarah's pulse picked up a beat. Her gaze flitted from one face to the next. There must have been two hundred pairs of eyes focused on her. And nobody seemed particularly pleased with George's announcement. Not at all. From where she stood, everybody looked pretty angry. One girl with long brown hair was snickering. A gang of scruffy-looking boys were shaking their heads. . . .

"Go *on*," George prompted.

She took a deep, shaky breath. "I think—"

"*You're* the Chosen One?" somebody snapped.

Sarah nodded. "Yes."

There were a few hushed whispers. The scruffy-looking boys leaned close, sneering.

"Bull," somebody else yelled.

Sarah's breath caught in her throat. Great. Nobody believed her. She looked like an idiot. She knew something like this might happen. It *always* happened. Everywhere she went, people laughed at her. Nobody ever took her seriously. Why not? Was it that hard to believe she was the Chosen One? Was she that pitiful? She didn't think so.

But she would show them. Just like she showed everybody else.

Amazingly, she found that she wasn't scared anymore. No. She was infuriated.

"Look at me!" she barked.

The whispering ceased.

She strode to the nearest bonfire. It was dying out, but it was still hot; she could feel it in the sudden tightness of her skin, the dryness of her eyes. A few flames danced on top of a sloppy pile of glowing red embers.

Without hesitating, she grasped one of the scroll's wooden rods and hurled it over the burning heap of wood.

The parchment unraveled and fluttered down on top of the flames.

Sarah held her breath. *Take a look at this, you jerks.*

The scroll didn't burn. The edges didn't even get singed.

No . . . the scroll created a fireproof carpet across the inferno, just as she knew it would.

A few kids gasped. Some of them backed away.

Steeling herself for pain, Sarah stepped out onto the yellow paper. Burning wood buckled and crumpled beneath her feet. She teetered to one side, nearly losing her balance. It was as if she were walking a tightrope. *Concentrate!* she ordered herself. Sweat began to pour from her brow. She gritted her teeth and inched up on top of the pile, keeping her eyes pinned to the parchment. But incredibly, the soles of her feet didn't even feel warm. Flames licked at the edges of the paper, but she was safe. A shaky smile spread across her face. She was doing it. . . .

"Oh, my God," a voice nearby whispered.

Sarah stood at the top of the pile and straightened.

Her gaze swept the crowd. Triumph surged through her.

This is what Moses must have felt when he parted the Red Sea, she thought. The derisive faces of those ratty-looking boys were now pale, open-mouthed . . . awestruck.

"I am the Chosen One!" she shouted. "I'll help you defeat the Demon! But you have to believe in me!"

Nobody said a word.

"The scroll under my feet is filled with prophecies that—"

"Wait!" a female voice interrupted.

Sarah scowled. *What now?*

A pale girl with jet black hair was squirming through the crowd. "I can help you!" she cried breathlessly, skidding to a stop in front of the fire.

"How?" Sarah demanded.

The girl flashed an eager smile. "Because I know everything about the Demon," she said. "Everything. She'll be coming back here. Believe me. And I can help you get ready."

Wait a second.

Sarah recognized this girl. She was the one who had stabbed Ariel. "How do you know she'll come back?" Sarah asked.

"Trust me," the girl replied. Her smile widened. "I'm her best friend."

"Her *what?*"

The girl chuckled. "Maybe I should say her *former* best friend. Back when she was Ariel Collins and I was Jezebel Howe." She beckoned Sarah to come down from the fire. "Come on. I'll explain it to you. Follow me."

Back when you were Jezebel Howe? What was *that* supposed to mean?

"Where . . . where are we going?" Sarah asked hesitantly.

"To meet somebody who knows even more about Ariel than I do," the girl answered. "The Demon's brother."

CHAPTER TWO

**Washington Institute of Technology,
Babylon, Washington
10:00 A.M.**

Trevor Collins felt as if he were walking into a tomb.

The cavernous room that had once hummed with eighty glowing television sets had long since fallen dark and silent. All of the equipment had been destroyed by a series of catastrophes and months of neglect. The dozen chairs were empty. His closest friends had either deserted him or melted into puddles of black ooze.

Nobody was left to repair the damage. Nobody was left to help or support him.

What did it matter, though? All of his test subjects were gone, too. So even if the intricate network of cameras still worked, he could only watch empty rooms.

Security was a moot point if there was nobody left to secure, right?

He sighed and padded softly across the worn carpet. The blank screens seemed to stare back at him like dead eyes. He'd poured so much energy into this command center, so much of his *life*. And he'd done it for a good cause, too—regardless of what anybody else said about him.

A familiar queasiness gnawed at his insides. He wasn't a bad guy, was he? No. He'd restored electricity to this campus; he'd provided food and shelter for dozens of kids; he'd devoted himself to finding a cure for the plague. But nobody ever understood him. He hadn't imprisoned those Chosen One believers because he was sadistic. He'd imprisoned them because he was willing to sacrifice a few lunatics for the sake of the entire human race.

But they aren't lunatics.

Okay. He'd made a mistake. He swallowed. How was he supposed to know that those kids *weren't* suffering from a mass delusion—that the Chosen One really existed? How was he supposed to know that ESP *was* possible, that some people *did* have visions, that there *was* a Demon? He was a scientist, an engineer. Not a psychic. He needed empirical data to support his beliefs. It wasn't his fault. . . .

Ariel.

He took a deep breath and glanced at his distorted reflection in one of the screens.

Never before had he hated the sight of his own face. But he looked just like her. Just like his sister, the Demon. He couldn't deny it: They both had the same long brownish blond hair, the same hazel eyes, the same narrow cheekbones. People used to think they were twins. Did that mean he was evil, too? Was he infected with *it* . . . whatever *it* was—whatever gave Ariel her awful supernatural powers? He clutched at his stomach. He was cursed, doomed—

"Trevor?"

Have they come to get me already? He spun

around, half expecting to see a knife-wielding mob. But it was just one guy. He stood in the doorway, silhouetted against the light: a tall, skinny boy with long, unkempt brown hair.

"Caleb?" Trevor whispered, flabbergasted.

The figure nodded. "Yeah, it's me."

"What . . . what are *you* doing here?"

Caleb stepped forward. "I didn't have anyplace else left to go."

Trevor shook his head. "I—I don't understand," he stammered. His eyes unconsciously flashed to the back wall. He used to keep a cache of rifles there—but the guns were gone. He needed to think. There was no doubt that Ariel's ex-boyfriend had come here to kill him. None at all. Caleb hated his guts. For all Trevor knew, Caleb probably blamed *him* for the fact that Ariel was the Demon.

"What do you want from me?" Trevor asked.

"I want to help you," Caleb said.

For a second Trevor could only stare at him. *"What?"*

"Look, I know it sounds kinda weird. But a lot of crazy stuff has gone down in the past couple of days, you know?"

Trevor nodded. "Yeah," he whispered shakily. "I know."

Caleb glanced at Trevor, then shifted on his feet, as if he was trying to figure out something to say. "Anyway, I've been thinking." He spoke quickly, avoiding Trevor's eyes. "You may not know this—but you and me have a lot in common."

In spite of his fear, Trevor almost laughed. What could he possibly have in common with a scraggly burnout like Caleb Walker?

19

"I'm serious, man," Caleb insisted. "Think about it. We're both pretty much alone, right? I mean, I know that *I* don't have any friends left. Do you?"

Trevor didn't say anything. He figured his silence was answer enough.

"We both got mixed up with Jezebel, too," Caleb went on. "We both know how much of a freak she is." He took a deep breath. "And then there's Ariel."

"What *about* her?" Trevor spat. "She's got nothing to do with me."

Caleb stared at him and shook his head. "That's not true. You know it isn't true."

"What's your point?" Trevor demanded. "Huh? I'm her *brother*. I can't help that. *You're* the one who went out with her—"

"Shut up," Caleb interrupted. There was a sudden edge in his voice. "I'm not trying to *blame* you for anything. I came here to try to work stuff out."

Trevor rolled his eyes, then slumped into one of the dust-covered chairs. "Work *what* out?" he grumbled, relaxing a little.

"I told you," Caleb stated quietly. "I think we can help each other."

"How?" Trevor glared at him. "How could *you* possibly help *me?*"

Caleb sighed and trudged across the carpet, sinking down into the seat next to him. Even in the shadowy half-light, Trevor could see that Caleb looked more haggard than usual. Dark circles ringed his eyes. He looked as if he hadn't slept in days.

"Did you know that the Chosen One is here?" Caleb asked.

Trevor's lips twitched. He didn't reply.

"Did you?"

"She's not here," Trevor whispered. The earlier nausea returned with a painful swiftness. "You're lying."

"I wish I was," Caleb murmured. "But I just saw her. She walked across this fire in front of your old house. Right into the flames, and nothing happened to her. Whatever powers Ariel may have, the Chosen One has got 'em, too."

"Walk—walked across a fire?" Trevor repeated.

Caleb nodded. "Yup. It was pretty crazy. As soon as I saw it, I bolted. . . ."

Trevor couldn't listen. If Caleb was telling the truth, that meant Trevor was dead. *Dead.* All those kids would tell the Chosen One that Trevor Collins had tortured them. They'd tell her that Trevor Collins was the Demon's brother. And if she really had powers . . .

"So I figure you and me are in pretty big trouble," Caleb said.

Trevor opened his mouth, but no words would come. He was shaking too much.

Caleb raised his eyebrows. "I also figure that there's only one way to save ourselves. We have to show the Chosen One that we've changed, that we're good people. We have to show her that we're sorry for the bad stuff we've done."

"And how the hell are we supposed to do that?" Trevor cried.

Caleb shrugged. "Well, you were trying to find a cure for the plague, right? Maybe—"

"I was trying to find a cure for the plague by capturing those Chosen One believers!" Trevor interrupted.

"So how do you think *that* will go over with the Chosen One herself? I didn't even *get* anywhere! I don't know a damn thing—"

"Just relax, all right?" Caleb snapped. "Jeez, man. Try not to get so worked up. You didn't know any better. You thought they were all crazy. So did I. So did a lot of people."

You're right, Trevor thought desperately. *I didn't know any better. I had no idea. I thought the visions were a symptom of the plague. I was just trying to learn.*

Caleb waved his hands at the dead video monitors. "And what about all these TVs and stuff? Is there, like, a college radio station here? I mean, we can try to contact somebody. We could even try to find somebody else who's working on a cure. The point is, if we just show the Chosen One we're trying to do the right thing, she might forgive us."

Trevor paused. *Contact somebody?*

That wasn't such a bad idea, actually. He certainly had the resources and equipment. This entire building used to be devoted to the study of communications. There was a CB and ham radio upstairs in one of the labs—as well as a telephone and fax machine. If he could get the electricity working again . . .

Strange. It had never occurred to Trevor that others like him might be conducting the same kinds of experiments. But why not? Washington Institute of Technology wasn't the only engineering school or technical college in the world—or even the country, or even the *state*. It wasn't even the best. So chances were pretty good that there *were* other intelligent kids

22

struggling to find a cure for the plague. Very good, in fact. Trevor had simply been too self-involved, too egotistical to see it. Ah, yes . . . but he knew better now. He'd been humbled by his mistakes. He'd *learned*.

And he would demonstrate his newly acquired wisdom to the Chosen One.

Hope began to well up inside him. Maybe Caleb wasn't as stupid as he appeared. He was an inarticulate slob—and drug use had clouded his brain, to be sure—but his plan might just work. He was probably *right* about the Chosen One. She would be a forgiving type, wouldn't she? Weren't messiahs supposed to be forgiving?

In any case, Trevor couldn't run away. It was too late. He figured he'd have to face the Chosen One at *some* point. Besides, he had nothing to hide. No. Even though he was the Demon's brother, he was nothing like Ariel. And if the Chosen One truly had supernatural powers, wouldn't she be able to see him for who he was—somebody doing his part, trying to save what was left of the world?

"So do you think it's worth a shot?" Caleb asked. "You think we should try to get in touch with other people out there?"

"Yeah," Trevor agreed. He slouched back in his chair. "Let's do it."

CHAPTER
THREE

**Mount Antero,
Colorado
11:30 A.M.**

Julia could feel her baby inside her.

A fleeting smile crossed her lips. *Yes.* Her baby was kicking.

She paused for a moment on the steep road and placed her hands over her globe-shaped belly. Even through the white cloth of her robe, she could feel the kicks; she could even *see* the jerky little movements—the tiny bulges that rose and fell. She felt a rush of childlike wonder. *A human being is growing inside me.* It was a miracle, wasn't it? At moments like these, she could almost manage to forget. . . .

"Julia? Are you all right?"

Luke. The joy melted away. No, she could never forget that she was alone with Luke. Any happiness faded in an instant, as if swept away on the crisp mountain wind. She could never forget the injustice, the terrible irony: *He* was with her, and George was dead. *He* had rescued her from being burned at the stake—while her baby's father, the boy she loved, lay in a heap of black nothingness back at Harold's farm.

25

And now she was stuck with Luke. She owed him her life. *Him!* The abusive monster who had robbed her of everything—

"Julia?" Luke asked again.

She raised her eyes—wincing at the sight of Luke's scabbed face, the awful blisters that stood out like dark leopard spots on his sickly skin. It served him right that he was no longer handsome. It served him right that he had caught the plague, that he had suffered. If only Harold had let him die . . . but she supposed she knew why he hadn't. Harold needed him. They were the same type of people: twisted and evil. And the Demon could probably use another like-minded follower.

"What is it?" Luke asked worriedly. "Is it the baby?"

No, it's you, she thought. But she shook her head and sighed. "I'm just tired," she grumbled. "My back is aching from all this walking uphill. Can we rest for a bit?"

"Sure, sure." Luke glanced up and down the lonely mountain highway. Either side was lined with an impenetrable wall of stumpy fir trees. "I, uh . . . I guess we can just sit on the road. Here." He swung his backpack off his back and gently laid it on the pavement at Julia's feet. "Sit on this. It's soft. It'll give your back some support."

Julia rolled her eyes. She'd had just about enough of the servility act. What was he trying to prove? It was all completely phony. At the very least, the real Luke had a spine, an edge. Why couldn't he drop the charade? Still . . . she needed the seat. Her bones were throbbing from the hike.

She let out a deep breath, easing herself down on the soft nylon cushion.

Ahhh.

But as relief spread through her tired body, she couldn't help but feel ashamed. Resting on this backpack was a sign of weakness, a sign that she *needed* him—in spite of her anger and hatred. What could she do, though? She couldn't survive in the wilderness on her own, even if she wasn't pregnant. She refused to give up. She would follow her visions at any cost. She'd made up her mind.

And if she had to rely on Luke to get her wherever she was going, so be it. She would learn the truth about Harold and the Demon and the Chosen One even if she had to sacrifice her self-esteem. She wasn't doing it for her sake. She was doing it for her baby's. For the *future*.

"I don't think it's too much farther to the top," Luke said absently, staring up the incline of the highway. "The trees are really short up here. That means we're really high up. After that, it'll be downhill for a while."

She shrugged.

Luke glanced back at her, swallowing. "You know, Julia—"

"Don't start, Luke." She groaned. "I'm not in the mood."

He blinked a few times. "Don't start what?" he whispered.

"Some kind of corny speech about how sorry

you are for being a jerk, how much you really love me. I don't want to hear it."

"How can you say that?" he choked out.

"Because you're a liar, Luke!" she cried, glaring at him. "How am I supposed to believe anything you say? Huh? You've been full of garbage since the day I met you."

He bowed his head. "But . . . I—I've been taking care of you all week," he stammered. "The Healer was gonna burn you. I got you away. Doesn't that prove anything?"

"No," she spat. "As far as I'm concerned, the only thing it proves is that you wanted to get me alone again so you could play your sick little games."

"Julia, please," he murmured, sniffling. He took a step toward her. "It's not like that—"

"That's close enough," she warned.

All of a sudden he sank to his knees.

She couldn't believe it. This was *way* too much. He clasped his hands in front of his face, as if he were praying. His blue eyes grew bloodshot.

"I just want to take care of you," he croaked. "Won't you let me? I don't know how much time I have left. I abandoned the Healer. The plague might come back again. I just want to make sure that you and your baby are safe—"

"Why is that?" she shouted. "I don't get it. Why do you want to take care of my baby? You're not the father. Doesn't that make you mad? Doesn't it bother you that I was intimate with someone else? I *loved* George, Luke. I never loved you. *Ever.*"

He shook his head. "I don't believe that," he whispered. "But it doesn't matter. I forgive you. That's the important thing. I just want to make up for it . . . for all the terrible things that happened between us."

Ha! *He* forgave *her?* That was big of him. Oh, yes. How *noble.* "They weren't things that happened between us," she said coldly. "They were things that you did to me."

He didn't say anything. His face grew pained.

"Why did you save me, anyway?" she demanded. "I thought you believed in Harold."

"I still do," he said.

Julia snorted. "So you believe that my baby's evil? 'Poisoned by the heretic,' as Harold would say? Come on, Luke." Her tone sharpened. "You're not making any sense."

"I—I don't . . ." He left the sentence hanging.

"Look, just forget this whole thing, all right? If you want to tag along with me, fine. I won't stop you. And the truth is, I probably need your help to get where I'm going. But don't think for a second that I'm going to have any kind of *relationship* with you. It's not going to happen. It's over between us, Luke. Forever. And nothing will ever change that. Do you understand me?" Her voice rose. "Am I making myself clear enough?"

For a moment he just stared at her. *Pathetic,* she thought. His vacant, shocked expression reminded her of a dog that had just been slapped. What was he doing? Looking for sympathy? If he only—

Uh-oh.

Her head spun. She gripped the sides of the backpack, suddenly very dizzy.

The earth dropped out from beneath her. In a flash she felt as if she were riding a roller coaster, plunging straight downward. Her heart jumped. She fought for breath. Was this a vision? Or was she sick? It was happening so fast. . . . She tried to call out to Luke, but she found she was mute.

No. Help me.

His body danced in front of her eyes in a kaleidoscope of multiple images. She saw seven of him, spinning crazily in the dimming light like water swirling down a drain. . . .

I'm in the room of darkness.

The Chosen One stands in front of the fire. I can't see her face yet. But I'm closer to her now, closer than I've ever been. If I reach out, I can touch her. . . .

"Look at the clock," she warns.

The hourglass stands in the shadows beside her, giant and terrible, its black sand nearly drained from the top.

"How can I stop it? Tell me!"

"Don't go to the mountain," she says.

"What mountain?"

She raises an arm and points to the blackness above the flames.

A beautiful, snowy peak appears there—dotted with greenery at its base, towering up into the clouds. It looks pristine, inviting . . . magical.

"Why shouldn't I go?"

"Because the Demon wants you to."

I'm very scared now. I want to ask more questions, but the flames are getting stronger. They're too hot. The sand is almost gone. . . .

"Time is running out. Remember the mountain," she says. "Remember to stay away."

Highway 90,
near Spokane, Washington
2:45 P.M.

This sucks.

Ariel was starting to get pissed. The highway was like an obstacle course. She couldn't gain any speed. Every few hundred feet another rusted heap of junk blocked her way. She must have passed ten thousand abandoned cars since she'd split from Babylon. Every time she accelerated, she had to swerve to another lane to avoid crashing. Why couldn't somebody clear these roads? Was she the only person left in the world with a working automobile?

Well . . . maybe.

But that wasn't the only problem. The other was the car itself. She hadn't exactly stolen *Motor Trend's* Car of the Year. Nope. The old blue Chevy was disgusting, covered with mud inside and out. And it *reeked*. The windows were cranked all the way open. Wind blasted her face, but the stink wouldn't go away. Whoever had driven this car before must have given up showering sometime last decade.

Then again, when was the last time *she* had showered?

Better not to think about it. No, it was too

33

depressing. She frowned, examining her pale hands on the steering wheel. *Yuck.* Her nails were caked with dirt. She ran her fingers through her hair and winced. It felt like a crusty old mop head up there.

Okay, as soon as she stopped, she would bathe herself. She glanced down at her grubby jeans. *Man.* She would also look for a change of clothes. She was beginning to feel like a cartoon character—somebody who wore the exact same outfit every single episode. Like one of the Simpsons or something. Bart always wore that red shirt, and Homer wore that—

"Jeez!"

An eighteen-wheeler appeared out of nowhere, stretched at a skewed angle across three of the four lanes. *No, no!* She frantically spun the wheel to the right. The tires screeched. Her body slammed against the door . . . but the car skidded past the back end of the truck, missing the rear bumper by less than a foot.

Ariel blinked. *Damn.* Her knuckles were an icy white. Her heart fluttered. She could have been killed—

Hold on.

No. She *couldn't* have been killed.

Her face twisted in a sour grimace. That was the whole reason she was speeding down this stupid highway in the first place. She exhaled and shook her head. Why had she even bothered turning out of the way? She should have just plowed head-on into that truck.

Nothing would have happened. Nothing at all. Maybe her body would have been thrown out the windshield and impaled on the truck's hood . . . but she would have just gotten up and dusted herself off.

Life was like a video game now. She choked back a laugh. The universe had become a giant Play Station. If she died, she would just get another life. Game over? Hit the reset button. Go for the high score. She glanced at the receding truck in the rearview mirror. Next time she wouldn't miss. No way. She would hit it, all right. A lump began to grow in her throat. Next time she would slam her foot on the gas pedal and gun the car up to a hundred miles an hour and crash so hard. . . .

Look at yourself. You're a freak. A monster.

How had it even happened? How did she become the Demon? A freaking *demon!* And when? Why didn't she feel *different?* Wouldn't there have been some sign—like the sudden growth of horns or a spiked tail, or the desire to kill everyone on the planet? She didn't want to hurt anybody. She didn't want people to vaporize whenever they got near her; they just *did.* It was beyond her control. She wasn't evil. Wouldn't she have felt something? Anything?

But I do feel something, don't I?

There was no point in lying to herself. She *did* feel a change. No matter how hard she tried to ignore it, that weird sensation lurked deep inside her . . . an undeniable feeling that something terrible was going to happen soon. She'd acknowledged it only once—in her diary, back in July. But from then on, she'd simply pretended that the feeling wasn't there. It was too scary. And she couldn't seem to pin it down or describe it even to herself. It was like trying to grab on to a puff of smoke, to form a sculpture out of water. It couldn't be done.

It all started when that Chosen One freak gave me the necklace.

Yeah. Somehow the damn necklace had turned her into the Demon. That was the only explanation. She glared down at it. Why the hell didn't she just take it off? Why was she so attached to it? It was just a dull piece of metal, shaped like a ticktacktoe board. It swung like a pendulum in front of her belly button. But she just couldn't bring herself to get rid of it. She couldn't throw it away—even though all the COFs told her it was cursed, that it belonged to the Demon. . . .

That's me, though, isn't it? If it belongs to the Demon, it belongs to me.

A wild urge to spin the car into the concrete divider flashed through her. But she wouldn't try anything stupid. No, no. She had a mission, a *duty.* She was going to put as much distance as possible between herself and the COFs. If they were all headed west to Babylon, then she'd just keep driving east . . . farther and farther and farther until she hit the Atlantic Ocean. Then she wouldn't be able to hurt anyone. Nobody would melt. Nobody would waste their time trying to kill her. Good-bye, West Coast. Hello—

Honk!

Her eyes darted back to the rearview mirror.

Dammit. There was a car right behind her: a vaguely familiar-looking red Honda.

Yeah . . . she *knew* that car. It belonged to one of

Trevor's old geeky engineering school buddies. That meant only one thing. Somebody from Babylon had followed her—

Honk!

So she was being chased. Wonderful. Why couldn't people just leave her alone?

Her grip tightened on the wheel. She stamped on the accelerator. The car leaped forward, mushing her body back in the seat. She snaked her way between two wrecks. The needle on the speedometer crept up toward sixty. The highway wasn't getting any clearer. No. But if she drove really carefully and maintained a steady speed, she might be able to lose this jerk in the maze of stalled vehicles.

She glanced in the mirror again. *Crap.* The Honda was even closer now—practically tailgating her. It looked as if there was only one person in the car . . . a girl with bushy hair. But Ariel couldn't see her face. What the hell did she want? It wasn't as if—

"Ow!"

Ariel's forehead slammed against the roof.

The seat bounced violently. Her insides were compressed, as if an invisible hand were pushing her lungs down into her belly. Her fingers slipped from the wheel. She couldn't see anything but blue sky. . . .

The car was flying through the air.

I must have hit something. . . .

Time jerked to a standstill. She was acutely aware of a dizzying weightlessness.

And then, very gradually it seemed, the car began to list to the left . . . tilting as its trajectory brought it closer and closer to the glittering blacktop. It was rolling in empty space, then *boom!*—her body smacked against the door.

Every bone on her left side buckled. She screamed in pain. A deafening rending noise filled her ears. She couldn't move. There was another terrible jolt, and she found herself sprawled on the ceiling. The car had flipped over completely. She squeezed her eyes shut. *Please stop. Please stop. Please—*

Silence.

Her eyelids fluttered open.

The car didn't seem to be moving anymore. Had she been knocked out? She couldn't tell. She tried to roll over, but her left arm was completely numb. A thick, intoxicating odor suffused her nostrils. *Gasoline.* With a grunt she forced her head up. She couldn't see a thing except thick black smoke. Her eyes instantly smarted.

Oh, jeez.

She coughed once. It was impossible to breathe. She tried to wave the smoke out of her face, but it was useless. There was no way she could find the door; she didn't even know where to *look*. She was utterly disoriented.

But maybe this was all for the best. If she was trapped in an exploding car, there was no *way* she would survive. She would be reduced to ashes.

Her muscles relaxed. Her brain swam in a pleasant red haze. No more oxygen, no more pain. She smiled sleepily, dimly aware of a hot tingle creeping up her legs. It felt strangely liquid. Was gasoline leaking onto her pants? Not that it mattered—

"Ariel!" a girl's voice screamed. "Ariel!"

Go away, she thought.

A metallic screech snapped her out of her reverie.

The smoke rushed from the car with an audible *whoosh,* as if it had been sucked out with a vacuum cleaner. Ariel blinked. The door was suddenly right in front of her, wide open . . . but it was upside down. Her face was inches from the pavement. Then it was *on* the pavement. Her cheek scraped against the uneven gravel. *Jeez!* That girl was dragging her out of the car! What was her problem? The car was going to blow up any second. Did *she* want to die, too?

"Come *on,*" the girl urged.

Whoa. Ariel's eyes widened. Was that *Leslie?*

"Oh, my God! Ariel! You're on fire!"

Fire?

Before she knew what was happening, Leslie's hands dug into her sides—half pushing, half dragging her across the highway to a sloping field. Ariel glanced down at her legs. Her jeans were in flames. She almost laughed. *Pretty trippy.* All the smoke inhalation was making her hallucinate. She pumped her feet. She could still run; her legs still worked. *Wow.* This was really cool. But just as she was beginning to enjoy herself, a shadow tackled her to the ground and smothered her, forcing her to roll in the spiky grass.

The hot, liquid tingle vanished.

"Hey!" Ariel protested.

She sat up straight. Leslie was right beside her. She looked awful. Her face was smeared with black stains. Her hair was a mess. Her lungs were heaving.

"What's going on?" Ariel muttered. "What are you—"

"Take your pants off," Leslie gasped.

Ariel blinked. "Uh . . . what?"

"Do it!"

Ariel glanced down at her legs again. The fire was out. Her jeans were black and shredded. A foul-smelling steam rose from the fabric.

"Fine, leave them on," Leslie barked. "Just lift the legs. I want to see if you're okay."

Holding her breath, Ariel bent down and rolled up the cuff.

"My God," she whispered.

The material was still very hot, but the flesh underneath was unscathed.

It wasn't even *red*. It was the same unblemished white it had always been. She felt sick. "Look at me. Nothing happened. Nothing—"

"It's okay," Leslie soothed, gently wrapping her arms around Ariel's shoulders. "Don't worry about it. We'll figure it out."

A tear fell from Ariel's cheek. She shook her head. "What's there to figure out? I'm the Demon. I can't get hurt."

"Stop it," Leslie hissed. "It's not true. You're *not* the Demon, okay?"

Ariel wriggled away from her. "Then why is this happening to me?" she wailed.

"I don't know," Leslie murmured. "But it's not your fault."

All at once Ariel was bawling helplessly. "Just go *away!*" she sobbed, burying her face in her hands. "Leave me alone!"

"No, Ariel." Leslie's tone was flat. "I'm not going to leave you alone. Not until I figure this out. I'm not going to let you out of my sight. That's why I stole this car and chased you. I'm not just doing it for you, okay? I'm doing it for *me*. For everybody."

Ariel sniffed and lifted her head. "What are you talking about?"

"Somebody's *doing* this to you, Ariel!" Leslie cried. "Don't you get it? The Demon put a spell on you or something. I don't know. All I know is that *you're* not the Demon. The Demon just wants everybody to think you are—"

"How can you be so sure?" Ariel interrupted. "How?"

Leslie shook her head. "Because I know you," she answered quietly.

Do you? Ariel wondered. She didn't even know herself. She glanced back toward the highway. The blue car was engulfed in flames, breathing black smoke. But the Honda was intact. So much for making a getaway. It looked as if Leslie would get her wish after all. She wouldn't leave Ariel alone. Nope. They were stuck together.

"How can you be so sure?" Ariel repeated. The words were barely a whisper.

"Let's just say that I have a pretty good idea who the *real* Demon is," Leslie said. "And her name isn't Ariel Collins. It's Jezebel Howe."

PART III:

September 2-20

CHAPTER FIVE

**Washington Institute of Technology,
Babylon, Washington
Morning of September 2**

"Hey, Trevor! It's me! The Artist Formerly Known as Jezebel!"

George cringed slightly. He stole a quick peek at Sarah. Judging from the sour look on her face, he could guess that she was thinking the same thing he was: *This chick is seriously messed up in the head.*

"Come on, Trev!" Jezebel shouted, marching ahead of them. "You can stop hiding. Don't be a wuss. The Chosen One just wants to ask you some questions about Ariel. She isn't gonna hurt you!" *Hurt you?* George frowned. Of course Sarah wasn't going to hurt him. And why did Jezebel need to *yell* so much? This Trevor guy obviously wasn't here. The three of them had been shuffling around the same dark, dusty corridors for the last hour, past science labs and empty classrooms, and they hadn't seen a damn thing. Why couldn't they just get out of this place? It was starting to give him the creeps. It reminded him way too much of school. He hated school. Now he remembered why he'd stopped going after the eighth grade.

"He must be upstairs," Jezebel muttered. She

45

paused for a moment at the end of one of the halls and shook her head. "I mean, I *know* he's here. I can feel it." She smiled at Sarah. "He's just scared of you."

Sarah didn't smile back. "Why? He hasn't even seen me."

"No duh." Jezebel rolled her eyes. "He's scared because you're the Chosen One and he's the Demon's brother. I bet he thinks you're gonna use some kind of strange magic on him and turn his blood to fire." She laughed. "That would be pretty cool, wouldn't it?" she added, turning the corner.

George shot Sarah another glance.

"Turn his blood to fire?" Sarah whispered, grimacing. "Where does she come up with this stuff? It's crazy."

"Beats me." George's eyes flashed back down the hall toward an unlit exit sign. "Look, Sarah . . . I think I'm just gonna split for a while, all right?" He spoke in a low, hushed voice. "I mean, we've wasted two whole days wandering around this town, looking for some guy who may or may not be able to help us. For all we know, he's long gone by now."

Sarah shook her head. "But you can't just leave me alone with *her,*" she whispered.

George shrugged. "Then come with me. But I'm getting out of here. It's a waste of time. I *have* to find Julia. Now."

"You'll find her soon," Sarah pleaded. "Come on. She *has* to end up here. You said so yourself. She's a Visionary. And talking to the Demon's brother could be important. If he can really tell us about Ariel—"

"Hey, you guys!" Jezebel called. "I found him!"

Great, George thought. He scowled. Talking to this dude was the last thing he wanted to do. Trevor was probably just as much of a weirdo as Jezebel. Or *more* of a weirdo. He was the Demon's brother, after all. Besides, everybody George had met so far in Babylon seemed to suffer from major mental defects—and he'd only been here two days. This town was by far the most whacked-out place he'd ever been in his life.

But on the other hand, what else did he expect? It was full of Visionaries. *He* wasn't the most normal guy in the world, either.

"Let's go," Sarah hissed. She grabbed his arm and gently tugged him around the corner. Jezebel was beckoning to them from a stairwell down another short hall.

"You sure this is such a great idea?" George muttered to Sarah out of the side of his mouth. He glanced nervously at the passing laboratory doors. "Didn't Jezebel say this guy was, like, a mad scientist or something?"

Sarah patted his back as they clambered up the steps. "Don't worry. She also said that he's scared of me."

George nodded. He hoped that was true. If Trevor had seen her little performance yesterday morning, then everything would be cool. He would fear her, all right. And if he feared her, he would help her. Sarah's problem was that she didn't realize how wimpy she really looked to most people—especially with those dorky-ass glasses and drab brown hair. The thing was, she *wasn't* a wimp. Not at all. Luckily at least

47

some kids knew what she could do. Ever since she'd walked across that fire, they'd kept their distance, gawking at her as if she were an alien or something.

"In here," Jezebel whispered. She waited at the top of the stairs with her ear pressed to a thick metal door. Her eyes narrowed. "He's talking to someone. He sounds really, really scared." She took a deep breath and knocked three times.

"Come in!" came a muffled reply.

Scared? George looked at Sarah again. If that was Trevor, he didn't sound scared at all. Hardly. He sounded really eager and excited.

Jezebel pushed open the door. "I *knew* you were hiding up here," she stated smugly.

"We're not hiding," a voice answered. "We're waiting for the Chosen One."

So they *weren't* scared. Once again Jezebel was full of crap. What was her deal?

George shook his head and followed Sarah through the doorway into a small room filled with computers and electronic junk. Two guys were sitting in front of a desk, fiddling around with an old-fashioned radio. It didn't take a genius to figure out which one was the Demon's brother. The guy on the left looked just like her—same hair, same eyes, same everything. The other dude was scraggly looking and burnt-out. He looked like the kids George had known from Juvenile Detention Camp back in Pittsburgh.

"Caleb?" Jezebel stared at the burnout with what looked like disbelief. "What are *you* doing here?"

"I came to give Trevor a hand," he answered,

48

glaring at her. "And to meet the Chosen One. I figured she'd come looking for us."

"Sure, you did," Jezebel mumbled. She gestured toward Sarah. "Well, here she is."

Both Trevor and Caleb smiled. Their eyes were shifty, though. The greeting looked a little rehearsed. Maybe they *were* scared. . . .

Trevor cleared his throat. "I just want you to know that I—"

"Get your kicks torturing people who believe in the Chosen One?" Jezebel finished.

His smile vanished. He turned to Jezebel. "What are you *talking* about?" he spat.

Hmmm. George frowned. The vibe in here was really tense. But he didn't get it. Did Jezebel want to start a fight with these guys? What had they *done* to her?

"Give it up, Trev." Jezebel snickered. "Stop trying to pretend like you're some kind of saint. Tell the Chosen One about the little experiments you do here."

Trevor's jaw dropped.

The other guy's face shriveled in disgust. "Have you been drinking?" he demanded.

Jezebel laughed. The grating sound of it set George's teeth on edge. "Come on, Caleb. Why is it that whenever I tell the truth, people automatically assume that I've been drinking?"

"Because you're not telling the truth, Jez," Trevor growled. "I don't get my kicks torturing people. I'm sorry those kids died, but I was trying to *help*—"

"Oh, yeah," Jezebel mumbled sarcastically. "I'm sure you're real sorry, Trev. Is that why you locked up all those—"

49

"Why don't you let him speak for himself?" George interrupted, as calmly as he could. "We don't need things to get out of control, all right? We just want to talk."

"*Exactly,*" Sarah stated.

Jezebel sighed and shook her head. "Let me tell you something about Trevor, okay?" She jerked a finger at him. "He kidnaps people. I should know. I was his first victim, way back in January. He held me at gunpoint and took me away from my friends. He made me pretend that I was his girlfriend—"

"That is such *crap!*" Trevor shouted, jumping out of his chair. His face suddenly grew bright red. The veins in his neck bulged. "You *chose* to come with me! And you made the first move! You told me that you *wanted* to be my girlfriend—"

"All right, all right," George said, stepping between them. This had gone *way* too far. "Everybody chill. None of your drama has anything to do with the Chosen One. Let's hear what *she* has to say."

Jezebel and Trevor kept staring at each other. Both were breathing heavily.

"Hey, Jezebel?" Sarah murmured. "Maybe you should just leave us alone for a while, okay? I don't mean to be rude or anything, but I just want to talk to Trevor alone. Is that all right?"

"No way," Jezebel snapped. She folded her arms across her chest. "I'm not leaving. You're the Chosen One. I'm gonna stay right here."

Oh, brother. George held his breath. This was perfect. Everything had to become a showdown with this girl.

"May-maybe I should start," Trevor stammered. "I just wanted you to know Caleb and I have been working up here all day. We got the ham radio going. See, we're looking for people like me—you know, people who are trying to find a cure for the plague." He spoke in such a rush that George could hardly understand him. "But something strange is happening. All we've received so far is this." He turned back to the radio and twisted a knob. There was a buzzing hiss as the volume rose.

"Believers!" a tinny female voice announced from the speaker. "The Chosen One is coming! He heals all those in his path! Wait for him on the western slope of Mount Rainier! There you will receive his blessing!"

Trevor turned the knob again. The voice fell to an incomprehensible whisper.

"Receive *his* blessing?" Jezebel asked, scowling. She turned to Sarah. "I thought *you* were . . ." She didn't finish.

Harold, George realized instantly.

He nodded to himself. Yup. There was no doubt about it. He could smell the stink of Harold's pseudo-religious crap anywhere. Who else would claim to *heal* people along the way? George's nostrils flared in anger. Just knowing Harold was still out there, fooling people with this kind of garbage . . .

"It's a trap," Sarah stated.

George looked at her sharply. "What?"

"I've heard stuff like this before," she muttered. She began pacing across the floor. "Back when I was on a boat, coming to America . . . we kept getting

51

these radio broadcasts. But back then, it was commercials. Everybody thought that America wasn't hit by the plague because we kept hearing the same dumb commercials, over and over. It was a trap to bring people here—to kill them." She hesitated. "I still haven't figured out *why*, though."

A trap to kill people. George swallowed. And Harold was involved. So if Julia was still with him, that meant she was headed straight for it—

"Um . . . *hello?*" Jezebel grumbled impatiently. "Anybody want to tell me what's going on?"

But George's mind was already miles away from the conversation. The tension had evaporated—replaced instantly by cold terror. Julia was never going to make it to Babylon, was she? No. Not if Harold could help it. He was leading her straight to her own grave. She was as helpless as a dog on his leash. And if George didn't find her . . .

"Where's Mount Rainier?" he demanded.

Jezebel glanced at him. "About a hundred miles south of here. Why—"

"I've gotta go." Without thinking, he bolted out into the hall.

"Wait!" Sarah called. "George!" She dashed after him and grabbed his arm, wrenching him to a stop at the top of the stairs. "Hold on," she cried breathlessly. "You can't just—"

"Let me go, Sarah," he interrupted. He yanked free of her. "I'm sorry. You don't understand. Julia's gonna die if I don't find her in time."

Sarah shook her head. Her face was creased with worry. "But—but—"

"Don't worry. I'll be back as soon as I find her."
His eyes darted to the open door. He leaned close to
Sarah's ear. "Just be careful, okay? Keep an eye on
that chick Jezebel. I don't trust her. I don't trust any
of these people."

"I . . . I . . ." For once Sarah was at a loss for
words.

George bit his lip. He wanted to say something
else—to wish her luck, to tell her how much he admired
her . . . but he'd never been good at things like that.

So he turned and ran down the stairs, without
even so much as a good-bye.

She'll understand, he told himself as his footsteps
reverberated down the dark corridor. *She always does.*

Babylon,
Washington
September 3-8

I can't believe George is really gone.

I feel like I've lost another brother. We spent every single day of an entire month together. We <u>confided</u> in each other. At some points in our trip, I felt as close to George as I ever felt to Josh. I know that sounds strange, but it's true. I loved them both in the same way. I wanted to protect George, too — to shield him and nurture him.

I've been thinking a lot about him, and one image keeps coming to mind: geodes. I haven't thought about

55

those rocks since I was a kid, the rocks with the crystals inside. But he was just like a geode . . . an amazing, glittering interior that was concealed by a hard and callous stone shell. I wish I could have told him.

I have to respect his decision, though. He was in love. He had a right to do anything he wants to save his girlfriend.

I wonder why I keep thinking about him in the past tense. For some reason I can't even articulate, I have an awful feeling he'll never come back. I guess it's a premonition. It's funny. A year ago I would have associated a word like ~~premonition~~ with crazy people — ~~people~~ who refused to see the truth ~~because~~ they were self-deluded.

56

Now I'm the craziest person in the world.

Even if George does find his girlfriend, he might wind up dead at the hands of Harold, or the Demon, or any number of people. Or he might just vaporize.

I suppose I should be used to losing people now, though. But it doesn't get any easier. First I lost all my family and friends when everybody melted on New Year's Eve. Then I lost Josh. Then I lost the one I loved: Abrahim. I lost him at the precise moment I realized my true feelings for him. And now George.

Poor Caleb. I'm really shaky right now. I just had my first long talk with him.

He was so scared of me. He says he and Trevor think

I'm going to judge <u>them</u> for all the bad things that Ariel did, since he was her boyfriend and Trevor is her brother. I feel terrible. Where did he get that idea? I didn't even <u>know</u> he was her boyfriend. He also told me the truth about Ariel — how she murdered her own mother when she was seven, how everybody says she's always been selfish and evil.

But most important, he says she underwent some kind of dramatic change in April. People started melting around her. She lost all her friends except one — a girl named Leslie.

The prophecies for the fourth lunar cycle state that "the Demon assumes a human form." It fits perfectly. The Demon possessed Ariel in

April. An evil being took the body of an evil person.

Another day, and still no sign of Ariel. I don't understand it. For once the Prophecies seem to be wrong. Ariel is supposed to be following me around right now. But the only person following me around is Jezebel. She's driving me insane. She won't leave me alone. I literally have to shut myself in the bathroom to study the scroll. George was right when he said I shouldn't trust her. Something is definitely wrong with her.

For one thing, she talks nonstop—mostly about Ariel and Caleb. Apparently she's wanted to kill Ariel ever since they were kids. The way she talks makes me really uncomfortable. It's like listening to somebody scratch their fingernails on a chalkboard. All I want to do is clamp my hands over my ears.

But this business with Caleb is <u>really</u> strange. She talks about him as if he's her boyfriend. I haven't seen them alone together yet, though. Not once. From what I can tell, he avoids her. He just sits up in that lab with Trevor all day, trying to get the communications equipment to work—to transmit as well as receive. And when he does talk to Jezebel, he doesn't look happy about it. So what's her story?

<u>Help me</u>! I'm going insane. I have to do something about Jezebel. Why can't she take a hint? Doesn't she know that

I don't like her? Everybody else leaves me alone, even the Visionaries. _Especially_ the Visionaries. I told them I won't talk to any of them until I'm ready. They respect that. They don't pester me about my reasons. _Unlike_ Jezebel.

I have to figure out the entire scroll before I talk to anyone. I have to crack the code. But I can't concentrate with her around. She's interfering with the most important thing in the world, and she doesn't even realize it. Her life depends on this, too! If I don't finish soon, we're all dead. George told me that time is running out, that we only have a few more months. Then something bad is going to happen. And I'm the only one who can prevent it.

Every time I try to work, Jez asks me all these stupid questions, like, "What does 'cut the pie and save it' mean?" If I _knew_ that, I wouldn't be so anxious, would I? And she keeps asking me what's going to happen on 9/9/99. How should I know? It's almost as if she _wants_ me to screw up.

I'm going to ask Trevor to lock Jezebel _out_ of this campus. It's the only solution. For all of us.

I'm scared. I asked Trevor to keep Jezebel away from me, and he said he couldn't. He says no matter what he does, she always gets her way. She has powers he can't even understand.

But that's not the scary part. The scary part is that she didn't _always_ have these powers. She used to ~~be~~ just a normal girl, although she was always a "manipulative bitch" in Trevor's words. And then one day she changed. Completely. She was able to read Trevor's thoughts. And she started saying that she wasn't Jezebel anymore. On that first day she told Trevor: "You won't know who I am until it's much, much too late."

That day was in April.

So it got me thinking. I don't want to make any assumptions ~~before~~ I have all the facts, but I can't help it. The journalist inside me is dead.

I think that we've all made a mistake.

I think that Ariel might not ~~be~~ the Demon. I think Jezebel is. And Jezebel might ~~be~~ "weaving magic to draw attention

63

away from herself" —just like it says in the Prophecies. It would explain a lot of things, including why Ariel ran off with our car. She ~~doesn't~~ have magic powers. Jezebel does.

Of course, it's just a theory. I can't prove it. Not yet. But the more time I spend with Jez, the more it fits. She definitely follows me around. She definitely fills my head with lies. Yesterday she told me that she moved into WeIJ with Trevor ~~because~~ Ariel left her in the snow to die. A week ago she told me that it was ~~because~~ Trevor kidnapped her at gunpoint.

Neither is true. I managed to ditch her long enough to ask Trevor about it. He said ~~Jezebel~~ was the one who left ~~Ariel~~ to die in the snow. It wasn't even snow. It was freezing rain.

Everything she says is a lie.

Still, Trevor is positive that his sister is the Demon. So is Caleb. I haven't argued with them about it—I'm still not certain that Ariel isn't the Demon. The only time I ever saw her, she should have been killed. I saw Jezebel stick a knife in her heart with my own eyes.

But if Jezebel is the Demon, wouldn't she be able to use magic to keep Ariel alive?

That's what really scares me. If she has all these powers, how can I possibly protect myself from her? How can I possibly defeat her?

All I can do is pray that I find the answer in the scroll—and, of course, that Jezebel will leave me alone long enough to do it.

Mount Peale,
Utah
September 9

"Harold? Harold, are you listening to me? Some of the Visionaries want to talk to you. They're . . . well, I hate to say it, but they're getting a little anxious."

Dr. Harold Wurf stared vacantly into space. From this snowy perch high above the green valley, he could see almost a dozen mountaintops. Unfortunately he was unable to appreciate the scenic beauty. No—in fact, he could hardly breathe. The air was too thin at this altitude. He felt so peculiar: light-headed and grouchy. Why did Linda insist that they climb *over* this peak? Wouldn't it have been easier to go *around* it? Maybe he should stop catering to her so much. It certainly hadn't gotten him anywhere. He hadn't even kissed her. . . .

Linda cleared her throat. "If you want—"

"I'll talk to them in a minute," he grumbled. For the first time in a while, he wasn't in the mood to listen to her droning British accent. He glanced at her, standing bundled at the mouth of a path that led down to the campsite several hundred feet below—where the rest of his flock was packing and preparing for another day's journey westward. Surprisingly, he

67

didn't even feel like *looking* at her. No. Her cheeks were too rosy; her eyes were too watery from the cold. And he certainly didn't feel like dealing with a bunch of impatient ingrates. "Go tell them that I need a few moments to myself."

"Are you sure?" she asked. She bounced up and down on the balls of her feet to keep warm. "I think I have a better idea."

Harold raised his eyebrows. "Oh, you do?" His tone was flat. "What's that?"

She smiled. "I think we should let them go. I think we should make an example of them. That way we can quash the last of the doubters."

Doubters. The word brought a bitter taste to Harold's mouth. Over the past nine months he had learned a great many things about adolescent behavior. Luckily, for the most part, he found that teenagers were ignorant and easily manipulated. They were blind to their own contradictions. They claimed individuality to be the highest virtue, yet almost all of their decisions were based on the whims of a mob. Peer pressure governed their moral code. But they also desperately craved vindication from an outside party . . . somebody who embodied everything they desired for themselves: power, physical attractiveness, genius.

In short, their weaknesses served Harold very well.

But there was one problem—one shortcoming specific to teenagers that continually caused him trouble. And that was their short attention spans. No matter how many miracles he performed, his followers always seemed to forget them. It was the old cliché: *What have you done for me lately?* Whenever *one* minor accident occurred, whenever there was *one* trivial setback, Harold suddenly found himself in a tenuous position. So two weeks ago, when that freak earthquake injured several members of his flock and allowed Julia and Luke to escape—

"Harold?" Linda asked.

He glowered at her. "What?"

"What do you think of my plan?"

"What plan?" he muttered. "It doesn't make any sense. How would letting the Visionaries go quash the doubters? Wouldn't it have the opposite effect? Wouldn't it show the flock that I had no control over them?"

Linda's smile widened. "Not if they all died."

Harold blinked a few times. He wasn't sure he'd understood her correctly. "What? What are you talking about?"

She sighed. "Are *you* starting to doubt yourself?"

Doubt myself? His forehead wrinkled. Maybe the oxygen *was* too scarce up here. . . .

"What happens to the people who doubt you, Harold?" Linda asked. "What *always* happens?"

He frowned. Now she sounded like a sixth-grade schoolteacher. Since when did she have the right to address him so disrespectfully, to pose idiotic rhetorical questions? *She* was *his* follower. He took a deep breath, struggling to clear the fog from his mind. Linda had become spoiled. That was the problem. She, too, was an adolescent. He had to keep reminding himself of that. And she was the only

69

member of his flock who continued to call him by his given name. Everyone else called him Healer—a title befitting the Chosen One. True, she was his greatest asset, the most powerful Seer among his followers, certainly the most beautiful . . . but perhaps she'd enjoyed a special status for too long. She was *not* his equal.

"You're implying that all the nonbelievers die," Harold stated. "And that *was* true, until the earthquake. Julia Morrison's escape proves you wrong."

Linda waved her hand dismissively. "That was a fluke, a case of bad timing—"

"A fluke?" Harold cried. "She was all tied up, ready to be burned—and an earthquake just *happened* to strike at that moment? Don't you think you're being a little naive? *You're* the one who insists that the Demon's power grows inside Julia as her baby grows." His voice rose to a shout. "So wouldn't the Demon want to protect that baby?"

"I—I'm sorry," Linda stammered quietly. She bowed her head. "I was wrong to think that a heretic could have escaped from you without the Demon's help. But you're more powerful than the Demon. I know something terrible will happen to the Visionaries if you let them go. I can *feel* it. Your wrath will destroy them. Trust me."

Harold sniffed. This argument served no purpose. He had no choice but to trust her, to let the Visionaries go. If he didn't, he would lose them, anyway. Their anxiety and resentment would grow inside them—and eventually they, too, would rebel or make their escape. Better to dismiss them now, to make it seem to the others as if he *wanted* hem tc leave. Yes. He had to appear strong.

For *everyone*.

"Can you see them?" Linda asked. She leaned close to Harold and pointed down at a lone road, miles away, amid the greenery on the valley floor. "A f.w others ran to catch up with them. I think there are about thirty altogether."

Harold hunched over the precipice and squinted in the direction of Linda's outstretched arm. Yes, he saw them, all right: a thin line of brightly colored dots against the gray of the pavement. From here they looked more like a single organism than a group of people, plodding away like some kind of inch-worm. They were hiking so slowly that he could barely perceive any motion. But they were most certainly *alive*. No magic had struck them dead yet—and it was getting late. The sun had already sunk below the mountains to the west, tinting the snow and clouds with a golden orange light.

"This is tedious, Linda," he said with a groan. "I want to go back to the campsite. I'm tired. I haven't eaten a thing all day. It's not healthy to stay so high up for so long."

Linda shook her head. "That's not true," she murmured absently. "It builds endurance in the lungs."

Harold glared at her. "Who *cares?*" he barked. "Is that why you insisted we climb this mountain? We're not in training, Linda. We're trying to head west as fast as possible. We're trying to stop the Demon. You know what? I don't blame those Visionaries for getting impatient." He paused, struggling to catch his breath. Even yelling knocked the wind out of him. *"I'm* impatient, too," he gasped.

"I have my reasons for wanting to reach this spot," Linda stated. "I'm a Visionary, Harold. Always remember that. I can see things that . . ." Her voice was lost in a low rumble.

"What?" Harold demanded. "Speak up."

Linda's mouth kept moving, but he couldn't discern the words. The rumble didn't die down. It swelled in volume until he could feel the earth beneath him vibrating. His eyes darted around the edge of the cliff. A twinge of panic shot up his spine. Was this another earthquake? Would he lose *more* followers? He shot a frightened glance at Linda. But she hadn't even flinched. She was staring at the opposite mountain with a wide-eyed, glazed smile . . . almost a look of rapture.

What the hell?

He turned to follow her gaze. His eyes narrowed.

Something strange was happening on the upper part of the far slope. The snow there appeared to be blurry and indistinct—as if he were looking at it through an unfocused camera lens. He blinked a few times. But there was nothing wrong with his eyes. Everything else looked perfectly crisp. The fuzziness began to expand, spreading down the mountain in slow motion . . . almost *dripping.*

He glanced back at Linda.

She smiled at him and mouthed a single word.

"Avalanche."

My God. Of course. His pulse quickened. He craned

his neck, peering back down at the valley floor. The tiny polka-dot line of nonbelievers had reversed direction, snaking its way back up the road. Their movement was only slightly faster, still excruciatingly slow—but he knew those kids must have been sprinting, scrambling for their lives in terror.

The tumbling snow gained momentum.

He held his breath. A deafening roar filled his ears. His bones were shaking. He could see now that avalanches had struck *all* of the mountains. The waves of snow turned a filthy grayish brown as they surged toward the valley, faster and faster . . . until they converged over the forest—completely smothering the trees, the road, and the Visionaries in a horrifying thunderclap of exploding rock and liquid.

"What did I tell you?" Linda cried. She whooped with laughter. "What did I tell you?"

The echoing blast began to fade. Within seconds the mountain range was still and silent. Pent-up air exploded from Harold's lungs. His jaw hung slack. He blinked a few times. A grayish white cloud billowed from the valley, obscuring his view. But he didn't need to see anything more. There was nothing more *to* see. The nonbelievers were dead—their lives snuffed out in the blink of an eye. He wanted to say something, but he didn't even know where to start. How had it happened? How did Linda *know?*

"Come on, Harold," she said, patting his back. She didn't even sound the slightest bit ruffled. Her tone was very businesslike, as if she had just received confirmation of an appointment. "It's time to address your flock."

* * *

73

Fortunately, by the time Harold convened his followers, he was feeling far more relaxed.

Euphoric, even. Yes, yes. His anger toward Linda had disappeared. How could he harbor any ill feelings toward her? Once again she'd predicted the fate of his detractors with deadly accuracy. She had a *right* to be treated better than the others. And if she wanted to call him Harold, she had every right to do that as well. It was his name, after all.

Night had long since fallen. The moon was very bright. He didn't even need a fire to illuminate the grim faces of his flock. He didn't want one, either. The dim, natural light was far more dramatic—especially with the mountains silhouetted against the star-filled, purplish sky . . . surrounding the campground like a fortress of black walls.

"People of the Chosen One!" he cried from the crest of a small hill. "Listen to me, and listen well! Today you witnessed another triumph over the forces of evil. You saw the Demon's work destroyed. You saw how the weak-minded were led astray, torn from the path of righteousness . . . only to be wiped out in an onslaught of—"

"I just had a vision!" Linda cried.

Harold paused, squinting into the crowd. *What's this?*

She scurried up the slope and joined Harold at his side. "Listen!" she shouted breathlessly. "I know exactly where we need to go!"

"You do?"

"Yes! I saw it! It appeared over your head as you were speaking. A mountain . . . a glorious mountain, almost twice the size of these around us." She waved her hands at the peaks. "It's in the state of Washington. Mount Rainier!" Her gaze swept over the stunned rabble. "We have to spread the word to go to Mount Rainier!"

Harold gaped at her. "I don't understand."

"*That's* where you'll face and defeat the Demon!" she cried. "And that's where you'll bestow your blessing upon the faithful!"

"My—my blessing?" he stammered.

She nodded vigorously, then threw back her head, as if she were caught in the throes of some kind of ecstatic trance. "The blessing of immortality!"

The crowd gasped.

Harold stroked his chin, struggling to process the new information. What did it *mean?* Mount Rainier? Nobody had mentioned that location before. The Visionaries had only talked vaguely about going west . . . but if Linda was confident that some triumph would occur there— well, then it *would*. He needed to relax, to wipe the confusion and surprise from his face. The flock couldn't know that he was as baffled as they were. And there was obviously nothing to fear. On the contrary, in fact. This sounded like the best news yet.

"We'll split up and head in every direction!" Linda shouted. "We'll spread the word to the faithful! In two months' time we'll reunite at the base of Mount Rainier. And from that moment on, we'll live forever!"

**Bicknell,
Utah
Night of September 9**

At first Julia wasn't sure she was awake. Everything was pitch-black. Her eyes were open, but they might as well have been closed.

Where am I? She couldn't seem to remember . . . yet she quickly became conscious of something else: cold. Her legs were freezing. And *wet*. She reached out in the blackness to touch them—and her fingers struck powdery snow. She tried to kick. Nothing happened.

Oh, no. All at once she realized she was buried from the waist down. She couldn't move.

"Julia!" Luke's panicked voice floated out from the nearby darkness. "Julia, can you hear me? Are you okay?"

"Yeah," she whimpered. But she *wasn't* okay. Something was dreadfully wrong. Her mouth felt dry, swollen. Her heart thumped painfully in her chest. "What's going on?"

"The avalanche must have knocked you out." His words were shaky. He took a deep breath. "I've been screaming your name for, like, five minutes."

Avalanche? The word struck a terrifying chord

inside her . . . and she wasn't even sure why. There was an awful blank spot in her mind. Had she almost been *killed?*

She chewed her lip, fighting to recall what had happened. Luke had been building a fire. Yes. She remembered that. They were tired. They wanted to stop for the night. The mountains went on seemingly without end. Whenever they conquered one, another stood behind it—one more in a perpetual series of exhausting hikes. And she didn't simply dread the pain and fatigue: the climbs that sent burning spasms through her back, the descents that turned her ankles to jelly. No. She dreaded accidentally coming across that one *particular* peak, the one she had to avoid at all costs . . . the one the Chosen One had shown her.

"Julia? Can you walk?"

"I—I—I can't even *move,*" she stammered. She struggled to turn in the direction of his voice. He sounded as if he were somewhere behind her. But she could only twist her neck so far. . . .

"It's okay. Just keep talking. I'll find you."

She swallowed. "I don't understand." Her breath started coming fast. She blinked several times, straining her eyes in a desperate effort to see something—but it was no use. "I think I'm blind. I'm scared, Luke—"

"You're not blind," he interrupted gently. "It's just all the stuff in the air. I think the avalanche must have kicked up a lot of dust or something. Don't you remember how clear the sky was? I was talking about how unpolluted it is out here . . . you know, because even when the sky is clear in New York, it's impossible to see more than a few stars."

That's right. She *did* remember that. Luke wouldn't shut up about pollution.

Okay. She nodded to herself. The rapid motion soothed her jangled nerves. So she wasn't blind. And even if she *was,* it didn't matter, right? Luke could see for her. Her inner pull would guide her wherever she needed to go, regardless of whether or not her eyes were functioning. She was sure of it. Even as she lay there helplessly, she could still feel that sensation in her bones—tugging at her insides, commanding her to get up and keep moving. It was more potent now than ever. It practically *consumed* her.

"Julia?" Luke asked. His voice was much closer now. His footsteps crunched tentatively in the snow. "Keep talking, okay? I want to find you."

"I'm right here," she called. "You're right behind me. Just keep moving in the same direction and you'll—"

A hand brushed the top of her head.

Thank the Lord. She breathed a long, trembling sigh of relief.

"There you are," he murmured. He crouched beside her, patting the snow around her sides. "Damn. No wonder you passed out. You're stuck in pretty deep."

She shook her head. "How . . . how did it happen?" she croaked. "The avalanche, I mean."

"Who knows?" He started digging her out, scraping the ground with his bare hands. "Maybe it had something to do with that weird thunder," he said with a grunt. "Remember those booming sounds we heard earlier in the day?"

"Yeah," she mumbled. But did she? Not really. Her memories of the past few hours were patchy and incomplete—like scenes from a movie she hadn't really been trying to follow.

"Are you sure you're all right?" Luke asked. His breathing grew labored. Bits of snow flew in her face as he feverishly scooped the debris away from her. "You don't sound so good. Are you dizzy? Do you think the baby got hurt?"

The baby! In a frenzy she tore her arms free and felt for her belly. But everything from her armpits down was still covered in layers of dirt, rock, and snow. And she was so cold that she couldn't even *feel* anything except numbness. As swiftly and gingerly as she could, she began to clear the debris from her midsection. *Let me feel you kick,* she prayed. *Oh, please, let me feel you. . . .*

"Relax, relax," Luke soothed. "Come on. You'll be okay. Let me just check something." He brushed her hands aside and pressed his fingers on her sopping-wet robe—right over her womb.

Julia stiffened. Luke hadn't touched her since . . . well, she didn't know *how* long. A silent voice screamed: *Get off of me!* He had no right to put his hands on her body. None. The mere thought of it filled her with disgust. Even if she were paralyzed and buried under two tons of rubble, *she* would be the one to make sure her child was safe—

"I can feel something moving," he whispered.

"Yeah, it's there." He withdrew his fingers and started digging again. "The baby's okay."

"Really?" she asked. A whirlwind of strange emotions spun her in a thousand directions. She felt relieved, *joyful* even . . . but also guilty and uneasy. Luke was evil. On the other hand, he hadn't meant anything by his touch. There was nothing remotely sinister or sexual about it. He'd genuinely wanted to make sure the baby was unhurt.

But had he really changed that much? Were his motivations really pure now? Part of her wanted to believe it . . . and another part knew she never could.

"You could feel it?" she murmured.

"I could," he whispered.

Wow. It was incredible. *She* hadn't felt the baby. She was too numb, too much in shock. But Luke had felt it—Luke wouldn't lie about that.

He stopped digging.

She could hear him beside her, breathing heavily, almost choking for air. He was working so hard to save her baby's life. And for what? So she could continue to reject him at every turn? Maybe she needed to step aside and take a good look at herself. Maybe she was sinking to his level—his *old* level. And she couldn't let that happen. An apology was in order. He *deserved* it. Despite every protesting instinct, she forced herself to say the words.

"I'm sorry," she whispered. "I'm sorry, Luke."

He didn't reply.

"Luke?" She frowned. "Did you hear what I said?"

But all she heard was the low howl of the bitter Rocky Mountain wind.

"Come on," she said with a groan. "Just answer me. I don't want to keep going through this." She reluctantly extended a hand.

He didn't take it.

Oh, please. She swatted blindly at the snow beside her.

And then she felt something. Something *hot.*

Her body froze.

Even in the blackness she knew what it was. The substance was unmistakable: gooey and sticky. It was the same steamy muck she'd felt once before—on New Year's Eve, back at the Jump Club in New York City. Terror washed over her.

No! She shook her head. This was impossible. She couldn't accept it. It *wasn't* happening. Not now.

Because if it *were* . . . it would mean that Luke had finally gone the way of everyone else his age. Quickly and silently. Without warning. It would mean that Harold's magical cure had worn off. But most of all, it would mean that Julia was stranded in the Rockies—alone and very possibly blind, with no chance of making it out alive.

That chance had just died with her ex-boyfriend.

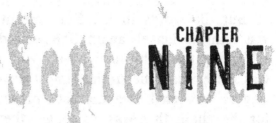
Motel 6,
Spokane, Washington
Morning of September 11

Don't freak out, Ariel kept repeating to herself. *Get a grip.*

Her eyes flashed over the small room again. She'd already searched the same area a zillion times. The necklace *had* to be here. But it wasn't on either unmade bed. And it sure as hell wasn't among the discarded soda cans and M&M's wrappers on the rug . . . or on the desk *or* on the big TV. She'd spent forty-five minutes scouring the bathroom, too. She'd even shoved her hand down the damn toilet. . . .

"Leslie?" she yelled. "Leslie?"

Nope. Leslie was gone, too. Wonderful. Ariel was losing her mind, and Leslie was probably out for a morning jog. The girl *still* had a bizarre obsession with health—even though they were living in some deserted hotel in a ghost town, and the world was probably going to come to an end any second now, and—

Stop! Relax! It's just a stupid piece of jewelry. It wasn't even yours to begin with. And it's evil. You're better off without it. You know you are.

83

But the words in her head meant nothing. She was lying to herself again. She seemed to catch herself doing that a lot lately. Well, why not? Anything was better than the truth. Almost unconsciously her fingers wandered over the back of her neck, feeling for the chain that was no longer there. She felt so *naked* without it. More than naked. It was almost as if a limb were missing.

How could she have lost the necklace? *How?*

She was wearing it when she went to sleep. She was sure of it. She remembered looking at it in the mirror when she was washing up. Didn't she? Of course. She *always* slept with it. She never took the freaking thing off. So this entire scenario was impossible. Utterly impossible.

"Agh!" she shouted. She stamped her feet. "Where did it *go?*"

"Ariel?" Leslie's voice drifted from the hall. "Are you all right?"

Finally. Ariel sighed loudly. "No, I'm not all right." She whirled around and stormed across the room, bursting out the door. "Where've you been? I've been looking all over for—"

Her mouth dropped open.

No way.

She blinked a few times, not trusting her eyes.

The strange-looking pendant dangled from Leslie's neck, standing out in stark relief against her black T-shirt. Ariel's stomach seemed to plunge. She felt sick—even though she supposed she should have been happy. She'd *found* it.

But what was it doing on Leslie?

"What's wrong?" Leslie asked.

"You're . . . you're . . ." Ariel swallowed and shook her head. She couldn't even form a complete sentence. Her brain was too muddled. "My necklace," she finally managed.

Leslie shrugged. "I was wondering what you would say," she remarked flatly.

What? Ariel shook her head in disbelief. That was it? She stood there openmouthed as Leslie marched into their room and dumped a shopping bag full of cereal boxes and canned spaghetti onto her bed. Until that moment Ariel hadn't even noticed Leslie was *carrying* anything. She couldn't tear her eyes from the pendant, glittering in the morning sunshine that streamed through the dusty windows.

"I found a grocery store not too far from here," Leslie mumbled. She flopped down on Ariel's mattress and leaned back against the pillows. "It's pretty much fully stocked. Can you believe that? We have all the food we can possibly eat for the next—"

"*Why?*" Ariel interrupted.

"Uh . . . what?"

"You're wearing my necklace," Ariel cried. "It's mine! Did it even occur to you to *ask* if you could borrow it?"

Leslie simply stared back at Ariel, her expression blank. "I didn't ask you on purpose," she said. "I knew you wouldn't let me have it."

"So give it back," Ariel snapped.

"No."

"*No?*" Blood rushed to Ariel's face. This was

insane. Had Leslie just been lobotomized or something? She wasn't acting like herself at all. The conversation didn't even seem *real*. "Give me back my necklace—"

"Ariel, listen to me." Leslie's tone hardened. "I have a *reason*, okay? Calm down and listen for a change."

Ariel clenched her jaw. All right. This had gone way too far. For the first time in a very long while, Ariel found she wanted to smack Leslie Arliss Irma Tisch. *Hard.* The chick needed a major shock to the system. Maybe they'd been living alone together for too long. Leslie didn't know her boundaries anymore. "You're pushing it, Leslie," Ariel growled. "You're really pushing it."

Leslie sighed. "You know what I was just thinking about?" Her voice suddenly grew much softer, almost wistful.

Give me a break. "I don't really give a crap," Ariel replied.

"I see." Leslie flashed a sad smile and sat up straight, hugging her knees against her chest. "I guess the honeymoon's over, huh? I was just going to say that I've been thinking a lot about that time I pulled you out of the fire in Seattle."

All at once the anger drained from Ariel's body—like dirty bathwater out of a tub. Why did Leslie have to bring *that* up? She really knew how to tell Ariel when she was overreacting. Borrowing a necklace was pretty insignificant compared to saving a life. And Leslie had saved Ariel's life many times. She'd *befriended* Ariel. And she'd remained a friend. Her loyalty never wavered, even though Ariel was a bitch, even though everybody else in the world wanted Ariel dead.

"Anyway, I was thinking, I probably could have left you in the lobby," Leslie went on. "Nothing would have happened. You would have just gotten up and walked out—the way you walked away from that burning car. I mean, you probably should have been dead from smoke inhalation by the time I found you. But you weren't."

Ariel lowered her eyes. She swallowed. The anger was gone completely. Instead a painful, lonely ache festered inside her. It was finally happening, wasn't it? Leslie was finally coming to terms with what everybody else had known all along: that Ariel was the Demon.

"What's your point?" Ariel whispered.

"My point is that you survived the fire in that hotel *after* you got this necklace," Leslie stated firmly. "*All* the weirdness started right then. So I'm thinking this necklace is what kept you alive all those times."

"I think so, too," Ariel croaked. Her voice grew strained. *Oh, God.* Now was *not* the time to start bawling again. "That—that's kind of what I've been trying to tell you. . . ."

"But it's more than that, Ariel." Leslie scooted forward on the bed. "I think that the necklace is almost like a drug. You're *addicted* to it—and you don't even know it. It's like you're addicted to its power. That's why you've never been able to take it off."

Ariel shook her head. "That doesn't make sense. . . ."

"That's because you're thinking like a *person,*" Leslie countered. "You have to think like the Demon."

I always think like the Demon, don't I? Ariel thought. *I am the Demon.*

"Just try to step back from the situation and look at it totally . . . you know . . ." Leslie frowned, snapping her fingers. "What's the word I'm trying to think of?"

"Objectively?" Ariel suggested.

"*Exactly.*" Leslie looked her in the eye. "Think about what the COFs said. Objectively. They said the necklace belongs to the Demon. Obviously they know that it has some kind of evil power. And let's just say for argument's sake that the Demon is Jezebel. If Jezebel wanted to make everybody think that *you're* the Demon, wouldn't she want you to wear a necklace with all sorts of amazing powers? And wouldn't it work even *better* if you got hooked on those powers—if you got hooked on the very thing that was fooling everyone?"

Ariel chewed her lip. Leslie's theory was pretty wild. A little too wild. She wasn't hooked on the powers; she *hated* the powers. Besides, how could somebody be addicted to a lousy piece of metal? And Jezebel hadn't even given her the necklace. Some COF had.

"The Demon wouldn't give it to you herself," Leslie continued, as if reading Ariel's mind. "That would be too obvious. And remember, it's not the actual necklace you're addicted to. It's the power of it—" She broke off and laughed quietly. "Jeez. Listen to me. I never thought I'd be talking about this crap. But Ariel . . . we both know it's real. And it's not *you*. It's *this*." She grabbed the pendant and held it up in front of her face. "You have to let go of it. So I'll hang on to it, and then we can go back to Babylon."

"No!" Ariel shook her head. "No way. I'm never going back there. Not after what happened."

"But you have to!" Leslie cried. "Don't you see? We'll go back, and everyone will see that without the necklace, you don't have all those powers. We'll prove that you aren't the Demon!"

Ariel stared at her. "Why don't we just throw the necklace away?" she wailed. "Why don't we get rid of it? It's evil. It's better if we just bury it somewhere and—"

"No," Leslie cut in. "If we throw it away, then we lose. Nobody will ever know that it was the necklace and not you. That way the Demon wins, right?"

Ariel sniffed. Maybe Leslie was right. Her gaze zeroed in on the pendant. Even now she still felt as if she wanted it back. Maybe she *was* addicted to it. The thought nauseated her. But what could she do? If it was true, she was basically a junkie. Junkies couldn't break habits on their own; they needed treatment, twelve-step programs, rehab. And that was for *drugs*—not some kind of twisted, evil magic.

She shrugged. She knew what would happen if they returned to Babylon. The COFs would attack both of them—and either Ariel or Leslie would wind up dead.

"I'm sorry," she whispered tremulously. "I can't go back there. I just can't."

Leslie stood up. "I'm not taking no for an answer, Ariel. Everyone thinks you're the Demon, which means the real Demon is just walking around somewhere and nobody knows it. So you *have* to show them all the truth. Not just for me. For yourself. And for everyone else who's still alive."

CHAPTER TEN
September

WIT Campus,
Babylon, Washington
Night of September 20

When Caleb Walker first found the mason jar full of homemade booze tucked away in one of the labs, he was pretty psyched. Yes, sir. Now he could enjoy a little nightcap. He chuckled as he hid the jar under his shirt. It might have looked like water, but he knew what it *really* was. Jezebel had told him all about Trevor's friends' dirty little secrets. They used to distill alcohol from apples. Clever, wasn't it? It made him feel better about himself somehow. Even geeks liked to blow off a little steam every now and then.

But when he headed back into the darkened hallway, he realized something.

He hadn't had a drink in almost three weeks.

Jeez. He stopped short and shook his head.

Not only had he gone without alcohol, but he hadn't smoked any dope, either. He'd been straight as an arrow. Amazing. He hadn't even *thought* about getting wasted. He'd been too busy trying to keep clear of Jezebel and helping Trevor build a two-way radio system. *He* had been living the life of a geek.

And it wasn't all that bad, either. In fact, it was pretty cool learning about circuitry and audio frequencies and ohms and all the rest of it. For the first time in his life, he felt as if he had acquired a real skill—other than being able to put a basketball through a hoop and gulp a whole beer in three seconds flat. This was grown-up. It was electrical engineering. It was *legit*. So did he really want to fall off the wagon?

He didn't think so.

The thought of that warm well-being was kind of tempting in a way . . . but the hangover wasn't. He'd forgotten how lousy he used to feel in the morning— the dry mouth, the nausea, the gross feeling that his brain was too big for his head and his skin was too tight for his body. He was sleeping so soundly these days, too. He could actually remember his dreams again, just like when he was a little kid. . . .

He pulled the jar out from under his shirt. He *didn't* want this. Nah. But he unscrewed the cap and took a whiff, just to be sure. *Blecch*. He nearly gagged. It reeked. It smelled like turpentine. No *way* would he drink this crap. He'd probably go blind. He glanced in either direction down the hall—and caught a glimpse of a sign marked Custodial Supplies. Perfect. This stuff would be great to mop the floors or disinfect the john. He hurried over to the door and threw it open.

"Hey!" a girl's voice cried.

He jerked to a stop, his heart pounding. It was the Chosen One. What was *she* doing in here? This was a closet. But she didn't seem to care. She was sitting cross-legged on the floor, surrounded by mops and brooms and buckets, hunched over that weird scroll. A single candle flickered on one of the shelves.

"Whew," she whispered. She patted her chest and offered a shaky smile. "Sorry for yelling. You scared me."

Caleb gaped at her, unable to respond. *He* scared *her?* How did she think he felt?

"So what's up?" she asked. "What's going on?"

"I was just about to ask you that," he found himself answering.

She smirked. "I was trying to get some time to myself."

His face reddened. "Oh, wow, I'm sorry—"

"No, no." She laughed and shook her head. "It's not *you*. I'm actually really glad you found me." She lowered her voice to a whisper. "Do me a favor and close the door, okay?"

"Um . . . okay." He spun around, clumsily bumping against the door with his shoulder. It slammed shut with a loud bang. *Oops.* His palms became clammy. *Mellow out!* he told himself. But he couldn't. It was so cramped in here. And being around Sarah made him really, really edgy. He never knew what to call her. Should he call her by her name? Or should he call her Chosen One? Somehow that seemed creepy—like she was a cult leader or something. Maybe he should just call her "ma'am." On the other hand, she was *his* age. Hard to believe. She acted a lot older than any eighteen-year-old *he* had ever met.

"Are you all right?" she asked. "Is something wrong?"

"No." He started fidgeting. The liquor swished in his hand. "I just, um, came to throw this out."

She peered at the jar curiously. "What *is* that?"

"It's, ah, well . . ." He swallowed. *Way to go.* Now she probably thought he was a lush.

A tentative smile spread across her face. "Is that *alcohol?*"

He hesitated, debating whether or not to lie. "I don't even really know. . . ."

"You know, I was just thinking I could go for a glass of white wine," she said absently. "My granduncle always used to serve white wine with dinner." Her smile widened. "It always upset my parents, too. They thought I should wait until I was twenty-one. They never understood the Israeli mentality."

Caleb forced an awkward laugh. He had no idea what she was talking about—except for the part about drinking. It looked as though the Chosen One liked to drink, too. Maybe he *shouldn't* throw this out. If the new messiah condoned an occasional nip or two, he should probably reconsider his newfound sobriety.

"Have a seat," she offered. She slapped the linoleum floor.

He took a deep breath, then eased himself down beside her. This wasn't so bad. He needed to relax. The Chosen One was pretty laid-back, even if she was a little weird. Then again, he'd known a lot of weird chicks in his short life. But she wasn't a *chick*. She was different, special, a leader. This was an honor. A lot of kids would probably kill to trade places with him right now, to sit side by side with the Chosen One. Especially the kids in *this* town.

"I don't think there's a garbage can in here," she said.

He stared at her, dumbfounded. "Um . . . sorry?"

She nodded toward the jar cradled in his lap. "You know, if you want to throw that out."

"Oh." *Duh.* He laughed again nervously. "That's okay."

Neither of them spoke for a moment.

"You know, Caleb, I've been meaning to talk to you." Sarah lowered her eyes. "And what I say to you can't leave this room. Okay?"

He swallowed. *Uh-oh.* It was a good thing he couldn't throw the booze away. A drink was sounding better and better. "Uh . . . sure."

"I don't want to offend you or anything because I know you're friends with Jezebel," she said. "But I wanted to—"

"I'm not friends with her," he stated flatly. "Sorry. I didn't mean to interrupt you. I just wanted to get that out in the open. I hate her guts."

Sarah opened her mouth, then closed it.

"Whatever she says is total garbage," Caleb added.

"Yeah. I've sort of gathered that." Sarah glanced at the scroll. "That's part of what I wanted to talk to you about. There's something in these prophecies. . . ." She didn't finish.

Caleb shifted uncomfortably. He hated talking about this kind of stuff: the magic, the idea that the future was somehow set in the past. His eyes wandered over to the crinkly parchment. He couldn't

95

even believe anyone could actually *read* that mess. It didn't look like writing. It looked as if somebody had blindfolded a bunch of hens, tied black pens to their claws, and let them walk all over the paper.

"Let me ask you something," Sarah said. She leaned over the scroll and ran her finger right to left under one of the lines. "In the past month has Jezebel ever said anything to you about the Visionaries?"

He shrugged. "I don't really remember. But I don't think so. I've been trying to steer clear of her."

Sarah nodded distractedly. "Yeah, I know." She grabbed the wooden handles and twisted them, turning to another section. "How about in June? Did you notice if Jezebel started becoming . . . I don't know, stranger? Or stronger in any way? I mean, Trevor told me that she could read people's minds and stuff. From what he says, her psychic powers really sort of blossomed in June. And other powers, too."

Caleb didn't answer. He felt too ill. He *had* noticed something strange in June, hadn't he? Yeah. He remembered the date because it was about a week before July 4. But he wasn't going to talk about it with Sarah Levy. No way. Because that was when Jezebel had come to visit him for the first time. That was when she'd forced him to fool around with her. And even though he'd tried to fight it, she still got her way. She *had* been stronger. . . .

"It's okay if you don't remember," Sarah said quietly. She patted his shoulder. "Sorry to bother you."

"No, no. It's cool." He hesitated, relieved Sarah had left it at that. "Can I ask *you* something now?

Why are you asking about Jezebel? Is she in that scroll?"

Sarah shrugged. "That's what I'm trying to figure out."

He stared at her. "What do you mean?"

"I don't know, Caleb." She shook her head and swallowed. Her face grew pale. "I don't know if you want to hear it."

"Yeah, I do." His pulse suddenly quickened. Something about the way Sarah looked, the way she was avoiding his eyes . . . he didn't like it one bit. "Tell me."

She turned to him. The light of the candle was very dim—but her eyes were unmistakably troubled behind her clunky glasses. "I'm going to be honest with you, Caleb. I know that you were intimate with both Ariel and Jezebel. And I don't want to offend you. But I think we were all wrong about Ariel. I don't think she's the Demon. I think the Demon may have cast some kind of spell on her to make people *think* that she is."

Oh, no. Bile rose in his throat. *Don't tell me what I think you're telling me.*

"You think Jezebel's the Demon," he whispered in horror.

Sarah reached out and touched his shoulder again. "I'm not sure yet. I just . . . I just wanted you to know what I thought."

He nodded. For a second he was worried he might yack all over her scroll. He had to get out of here. This little closet was *way* too claustrophobic. His knees were wobbling, but he forced himself to stand. "I . . . uh, think I'm gonna go."

"I understand," Sarah said soothingly. "Look, I'm sorry. I know you must be going through a lot of difficult, painful feelings—"

"It's cool," he muttered. He couldn't deal with any psychobabble right now, not even if it came from the Chosen One. Nope. He needed a drink. He didn't care if it tasted like cow piss, either. He reached for the door. "I'll see you later."

"Just be careful, okay?" she whispered.

"I will."

He closed the door behind him and leaned against it, squeezing his eyes shut. *What have I done?* His heart was pounding. He should have trusted his instincts about Jez. He *knew*—

"Hey, Caleb."

The jar slipped from his fingers. It crashed to the floor, splattering glass and putrid liquor everywhere. But he hardly noticed.

He whirled around—and found himself standing face-to-face with Jezebel.

"Drinking alone in a closet, are we?" she asked. She smirked and shook her head. "Tsk, tsk. Trevor's not gonna like that one bit."

He blinked a few times. *Okay, calm down.* His mind raced. She'd said he was alone. She didn't know the Chosen One was in the closet. She thought he was just getting drunk. That was fine. He could live with that. But he had to get her away from this door. *Now.*

"Why are you so nervous?" she asked. "I don't care that you're having fun. I mean, I *am* a little hurt you didn't invite me to join you. . . ." She eyed him suggestively.

"I was—ah, I was just going to find you," he stammered. He tried to smile. "Come on." He grabbed her arm and tugged her toward the lab where he had found the jar. "There's plenty more of this stuff back in—"

"Don't lie to me, Caleb."

He froze. "What?"

She shook free of his grasp. Her eyes grew cold. "You weren't going to find me. You were plotting *against* me."

"No." He shook his head. His stomach heaved. "That's not true at all." But the words were hoarse and simpering. They carried no weight. "I was just . . . you know, drinking."

"Sure, you were." She cocked an eyebrow. "Drinking in the janitor's closet. Of course."

"I . . . I didn't want Trevor to find me," he insisted.

Her gaze bored into his own, moving through him, obliterating him. "I know this has something to do with the Chosen One and her scroll," she snapped. "I *know* it. She's changed her mind about Ariel, hasn't she? She thinks *I'm* the Demon. She's been turning you against me since the day she got here. You and all the rest of the Visionaries."

Oh, my God. Caleb shuddered. Jezebel was talking about the Visionaries—just as the Chosen One said she would. His entire body started trembling uncontrollably. "You got it wrong," he whispered. "It's not true—"

"Oh, yes, it is." She smiled, but her eyes remained icy. "But don't worry. Sarah and her stupid scroll won't stand in our way again. Ever."

PART III:

September 21–30

The Ninth Lunar Cycle

In all of her many roles, in all the hoaxes she'd perpetrated, Naamah had never felt so pleased with a single performance.

Her false "vision" sealed the fate of a thousand Seers. The timing of the predicted avalanches had been perfect. Harold's power had been proven for the last time. And upon Naamah's command, his flock had split up in every direction to spread the word—scouring the western half of the continent for all those in search of the Chosen One . . . only to draw them to their own annihilation.

Of course, there might be a few doubters left, a few stragglers who thought they knew better than to receive Harold's blessing. But the Lilum's radio broadcast would take care of them—just as the phony commercials of the third, fourth, and fifth lunar cycles had led the Seers to the massacre in New York. Naamah could finally relax.

She and her hooded sisters were entering the

final phase of the countdown. The setbacks of the previous lunar cycle had been rectified. The plans were once more falling into place, weaving together like threads in a dark tapestry. No more mysteries lay ahead. No more accidents could befall the Lilum. Every prophecy for the last three lunar cycles would be fulfilled; every catastrophe hidden in the codes would serve the Demon's end—just as the avalanches had.

And soon Naamah would lay eyes upon her mistress for the first time.

Soon she would greet Lilith, face-to-face.

Soon she would embrace Lilith, flesh to flesh.

Only one variable still remained: the location of the scroll. But Naamah's fears about its whereabouts had begun to fade. If Aviva had died, then chances were good that Sarah Levy and George Porter had died with her. Any number of tragedies could have disposed of them—a car accident, a beating at the hands of teenage bandits, starvation. . . . It was pointless to speculate. The odds of the scroll's reappearing were negligible.

And so Naamah's journey as Linda Altman would

soon come to a close. The time had almost come for her to reveal her identity to Harold Wurf. It was almost sad, in a way. She would miss the excitement, the danger, the thrill of posing as another person.

Most of all, however, she would miss deceiving Harold.

The boy was an endless source of amusement. His delusions of grandeur knew no bounds. She couldn't wait to see the expression on his face when he learned the truth . . . about himself, of course—but especially about his unwitting role in the Demon's victory.

Fortunately she wouldn't have to wait much longer.

Lilith had chosen wisely all those millennia ago when she'd picked this continent as the site of her triumphant return. It was a land of unparalleled beauty: of glittering cities, lush forests, flat plains—and, of course, glorious mountain ranges. Every one of those landscapes had provided a setting for another victory. The disposal of the Seers had been an exquisite work of choreography, a dance of death on a global scale . . . all directed by Lilith's unseen hand.

The dance was almost over. The campaign that had begun on New Year's Eve was finally within measurable distance of its end. Paradise awaited Naamah and her sisters.

And only the Lilum and their pawns would live to see it.

ELEVEN

**WIT Campus,
Babylon, Washington
Morning of September 21**

"So what you're trying to tell me is . . ."

"Your sister isn't the Demon," Sarah whispered.

Trevor gazed down at the parchment spread before them. He struggled to accept her words. But he couldn't. They were as senseless as the gridlike formations of those Hebrew letters. He didn't even know what he *felt* . . . other than a prickling discomfort, a vague tightness in his chest. If Sarah was correct, then his life would literally be turned on its head. All of his beliefs—about himself, about his family, about his closest relationships—all of them would be proved false. And Trevor needed that foundation. He couldn't survive without it.

"Are . . . are—are you *sure?*" he finally stammered.

She sighed. "About ninety-nine percent sure. Otherwise I wouldn't have said anything."

This can't be. The unpleasant sensation in his rib cage intensified, tightening around his heart. He knew his sister was the Demon. He knew it as well as he knew anything.

"The evidence adds up," Sarah stated. Her voice was measured and quiet. "Jezebel's behavior fits almost every prophecy of this lunar cycle. Ariel isn't even *around*. And part of last month's prophecy said that I would break from the traitor—which I did. It also said that the Demon would counterattack with magic."

Trevor shook his head, unable to stop staring at the scroll. He felt as if he were lost in a labyrinth. And there was no possibility of escape. Another bewildering dead end lurked around every corner. "I just don't understand what you're saying," he muttered.

"Jezebel counterattacked by pitting me against *Ariel* instead of against herself."

"But how?"

"She used magic to keep Ariel alive when she stabbed her," Sarah explained. "I don't know what *kind* of magic, but I—"

"Then you can't be sure," he interrupted. The words seemed to come from someone else. Why was he arguing? Why was he clinging so rashly to the notion that his own sister was the Demon? He should be doing the opposite. He should be dancing for joy. He was so afraid, though. He couldn't face this. He couldn't admit to placing his faith in a lie—a horrible lie that sealed his hatred for the only surviving member of his family. Who could?

"The evidence adds up," Sarah repeated.

"But she killed my mother," he mumbled—as much to himself as to Sarah. "I saw it. She threw a hair dryer in the bathtub and electrocuted her." A lump formed in his throat. His eyes grew misty. "Don't you see?" he whispered in a hollow, quavering voice. "She's *always* been evil. Always . . ."

Sarah laid a hand on his shoulder. "I'm not saying your sister is an angel. I'm not even saying she's *good*. I'm just saying that she isn't who everybody says she is. And even if she . . ." The sentence hung in the air, unfinished.

Trevor turned to her. "Even if she what?" he croaked.

"Even if she *did* kill your mom, it has nothing to do with her being the Demon," Sarah mumbled awkwardly. "The Demon has only been around for five months—at least in human form. If anything, all the awful things Ariel did in the past would make her a more believable scapegoat. You see what I mean?"

I don't know. The seconds ticked by in silence. Trevor hung his head, unable to say anything else, unable even to look Sarah in the eye. Never before had he so desperately wished he were someplace far from Babylon—away from this dingy little lab, this campus, the stream of revelations that grew more horrifying with every passing moment. How easy would his life be if he were just a nobody in some small town, oblivious, idling the days away until he turned twenty-one and melted? It wouldn't be long now, though. Only a few more months.

I was duped. Jezebel seduced me. I underestimated her. I thought she was another frivolous, self-serving girl—somebody who could use me as I used her. But she manipulated me from day one. Me and everyone else in this town.

"What does Caleb have to say about all this?" he finally whispered. His voice was strained. "Did you tell him?"

Sarah nodded. "Yeah. Last night. He was pretty upset, too." She shivered. "Jezebel almost heard the whole thing. That's why I made sure she wasn't around here before I came to get you—" She broke off suddenly.

There was a clatter of urgent footsteps in the hall.

Uh-oh. Trevor swallowed. Maybe Jezebel *was* here.

"You guys!" Caleb shouted. A second later he burst through the door. He was practically hyperventilating—but there was a crazed, exultant sparkle in his eyes.

Trevor stared at him.

"Come upstairs!" Caleb gasped. "You gotta hear this. It's instructions for making a cure! They found it in . . ."

He scrambled back into the hall.

Holy— Trevor exchanged a dumbfounded glance with Sarah. Before he knew it, he was sprinting after her—out of the room, up the stairs, and into the communications center.

"Check it out!" Caleb cried, barely able to contain himself. He hunched over the ham radio. "Listen to this guy!"

Trevor's eyes narrowed as he and Sarah crowded around the table. At first he could hear nothing but static. But then Caleb turned a dial, adjusting the amplitude—and a small voice crackled through the speaker.

". . . add liquid extract of echinacea to the boiling water," it said. "Use one cup per four gallons. You are now ready to dump in the half pound of turnip roots."

Turnip roots? Was this some kind of prank? It had to be. Trevor's fleeting hope faded. How could Caleb be so gullible? He really *was* an idiot. For all they knew, this broadcast was connected to the message urging people to gather at Mount Rainier.

"Make sure the turnip roots are ripe, soft, and fleshy," the voice went on. "Canned rutabagas will not suffice, as chemical pollutants will—"

"Oh, my God!" Sarah shrieked.

Trevor flinched. "What?" he whispered, suddenly panicked. "What is it?"

"That voice!" she whimpered. She thrust a finger at the speaker. "It . . . it's my brother!"

Your brother? Trevor's gaze darted to Caleb.

". . . will now await confirmation," the voice said. "Please respond on ten megahertz AM. Over."

Static filled the speaker again. Caleb shook his head. He stared back at Trevor with an anxious look: *What do we do?*

"Turn it up!" Sarah yelped. A frantic smile appeared on her lips. She started jumping up and down. "Turn it up! Is there any way we can talk to him?"

"I . . . uh, I hope so," Trevor muttered, swallowing. Everything was happening too fast; he couldn't keep his thoughts straight. He didn't even know Sarah *had* a brother. And he still wasn't sure if the ham radio would transmit. He'd rewired the oscillator and hooked up a mouthpiece from an old CB, but still. . . . He hunched over Caleb. Ten megahertz (AM) was in the HF band—shortwave. So it was probably coming from another country, maybe very far away.

He flicked the transmission switch. The static fell silent.

"Hey!" Sarah cried. "What are you doing? I thought—"

"You can't broadcast and receive at the same time," he interrupted. "Sorry." He adjusted the outgoing carrier wave so that it matched that of the incoming signal. "That's why your brother said 'over.' He wants somebody to answer." He handed her the mouthpiece. "Go ahead."

"Josh?" she shouted. She grasped the tiny piece of black plastic so tightly that her fingers turned white. "Josh, can you hear me? It's Sarah!" She paused. "It's Sarah!"

"Say 'over,'" Trevor instructed.

"Over! Over!" she yelled. "Josh—"

There was a *click* as Trevor switched the radio back into receive mode. His fingers were getting moist. This was a little hectic. Sarah's hysteria was contagious. He held his breath. White noise gurgled from the speakers. . . .

"Sarah?" the voice asked after a moment. "Is that really you?"

"Yes!" She shoved Trevor aside and flicked the switch herself. "It's me, Josh. It's me! Where are you?" She jiggled the switch again.

"Russia!" the voice shouted, laughing. "I'm at this army base. . . ." His words were garbled in a high-pitched hiss. ". . . believe you're alive! Where are *you?* Over."

Sarah shook her head. "I'm in Washington," she replied, tears streaming down her face. "Oh, Josh," she sobbed. "I'm so sorry. I thought you were dead. I didn't know. . . ."

Trevor stared at her. He couldn't believe this. Who would have thought that the Chosen One would have a family reunion via shortwave radio? For some reason, it made him really uncomfortable. His ears shut down. He wasn't able to listen; it was too intense, too emotional.

He stared at the floor. *Ariel.* His own sister, his one sibling. The only family he had left. He couldn't get her out of his head. He hated Ariel, didn't he? But he pictured a dreamy scenario where *they* were reunited . . . where all was forgiven between them, where they rebuilt what they had before their mother's death. It didn't make sense. They were children back then, *babies*—young and foolish. Ariel had *murdered* their mother. And then—to his surprise—he found that his eyes were welling with tears, too.

Was the death an accident? He'd never given her a chance to explain herself. And he had to admit it; he knew he'd been wrong about her in other ways—

"Sarah, we know how to make an antidote for the plague," Josh announced. "Over."

Trevor jumped. He'd almost forgotten why he'd come running up here in the first place. This was no prank; this kid was the Chosen One's brother. Trevor wiped his bloodshot eyes and searched feverishly for a pen. They had to write this down.

"Go on, Josh," Sarah urged. "What is it?"

A few seconds of excruciating silence followed.

"Here's the deal," Josh finally said. "Those girls in black set off a bunch of Russian biological weapons. *That's* what caused the plague. A high amount of hormones makes teenagers immune. Don't ask me to explain. Luckily the Soviets invented a cure, too. . . ."

Biological weapons. Trevor nodded grimly. He'd figured as much all along. But how could hormones cause immunity?

". . . have to boil water—lots of it, maybe twelve gallons," Josh went on. "Add small amounts of echinacea. There's a naturally occurring chemical in the extract that bonds with something in the turnip roots at high temperatures. Toss in the turnips and boil them for, like, four hours, then dry the bulbs in the sun. It's going to stink, but—"

A loud *pop* cut him off.

Trevor frowned.

At first he thought they had blown the fragile sound system. But then he heard a quick *rat-tat-tat,* followed by muffled shouting.

"Josh?" Sarah whispered. Her eyes were wide.

A distorted, bloodcurdling scream tore from the speaker.

Oh, no. Trevor's face whitened. *Oh, no . . .*

Static filled the room. Nobody moved. Nobody breathed—

"Don't bother ringing this number again," a girl snapped in a clipped British accent. "It's out of service."

There was a final crack, and the channel went dead.

TWELVE

Route 90,
between Spokane and Babylon, Washington
September 22–29

September 22

So today I did something I never thought I'd do.

I poured sugar in somebody's gas tank. <u>Leslie's</u> gas tank, to be more specific.

I can't believe it worked. I was actually sort of proud of myself. (God, I really hope she doesn't snoop through this.) When she turned the key, the engine made this hideous grinding noise, and then the car just sort of died. Kaput. Here we are, stuck out in the boonies, several hundred miles from where Leslie wants us to be.

Man, oh, man. What a freaking relief.

She wanted us to go back to Babylon

today. I pretended to be sick for a
while to put it off. Well, okay, I didn't
really pretend. I ate some old tuna fish
in hopes of getting food poisoning.
Guess what? That worked, too. All my
plans are really coming together these
days. I barfed my brains out for about
twenty-four hours. I must have had a
fever of 105 or something. Seriously. I
was hallucinating. But now I'm fine.

I'm scared, okay? I admit it.

September 23

It was a big mistake to ruin the car.
Now we're <u>walking</u> back to Babylon. I
can't believe it. Leslie's totally psyched,
of course. What better way to keep in
shape than walk across an entire state?

I've been thinking a lot about the
necklace. I don't miss it anymore, though.
Not at all. It was kind of hard for a
few days, but now I'm totally cool. I

guess I really _was_ addicted. I just had to kick the habit cold turkey. Leslie can keep it, for all I care. I don't want to harsh her mellow, but for the first time I can really see how ugly it is. I always knew, of course, but now it's like I'm looking at it objectively (to quote Leslie's new favorite word).

Secretly, I've been paying extra attention to the way she acts, looking for changes in her behavior. But if the necklace is having any effect on her, I can't see it. She's still the same old chick. Funny as hell, a little out there, and totally into her own thing.

Like this afternoon, we found a wrecked truck full of old clown costumes. It must have been part of a traveling circus or something. Anyway, Leslie dressed up in this ridiculous yellow one-piece outfit with ruffles. It was like a hundred sizes too big. Then she ran around in circles, singing at the top of her lungs: "Figaro, Figaro, Figaro!" Vintage Leslie.

I don't know whether it's good or bad that she's the same. I try not to think about it too much. Better just to have fun, right?

Something really weird happened last night. I had the craziest dream. It left me with the strangest sensation. It's kind of like when you smell something good that reminds you of a nice thing that happened a long time ago.

I've been having a lot of weird dreams lately. They all began after I stopped wearing the necklace. Usually they're totally surreal, like I'm flying through the air or talking to somebody who changes into a hundred different people. And usually I can remember them really well. This one was different. It's all fuzzy and incomplete.

I was in a cave or something, talking to somebody who was my best friend. But the whole time I had my back to her. I couldn't seem to turn around. There was a big fire, and I just kept looking at it. I never saw her face. I didn't even know what she looked like. It wasn't Leslie, though. It was some girl who I've known all my life but never met. I know that makes no sense. What can I say? She was so familiar. We kept talking about something bad, something that's going to happen, but I can't remember what it was.

That _is_ pretty abstract. I sound like a total nutcase. Mental note to myself: forget what I just wrote. Forget the whole thing, actually. I probably just ate some stale cornflakes or something.

I don't know whether I should be ecstatic or scared out of my mind.

Today we met a bunch of kids who <u>left</u> Babylon. Mind-blowing, isn't it? For the past nine months everybody's been going <u>toward</u> Babylon. But I guess there's no reason to hang around there anymore once you've gotten to talk to the Chosen One.

According to these kids, the Chosen One has the cure for the plague.

At first I didn't believe it. But then one of them showed me his ID. He had really big black scabs on his face. He turned twenty-one this month. He says he started to catch the plague, but somebody came running over and stuffed this horrible-tasting root down his throat.

Then presto! He was fine. He also had a bag full of the roots, which he showed to us, too. I still can't get the stench out of my nostrils. It smelled like a toilet that hadn't been cleaned in forty years. This is the stuff that makes you live forever?

I was nervous the whole time, but none of them seemed to recognize me. Nobody accused me of being the Demon. Nobody tried to stab me.

Best of all, nobody vaporized.

So, hey . . . maybe those roots really <u>do</u> work.

Leslie, on the other hand, seems kind of doubtful. She says that we can't make any snap judgments until we're there and see it for ourselves.

But maybe that's just the necklace talking.

September 29

Tomorrow is the big day. Tomorrow I go home.

I still can't believe that Leslie talked me into this. Tonight we're just chilling in a nice secluded spot about five miles from Old Pine Mall, and I'd be happy to stay here the rest of my life. But Leslie won't hear of it. We <u>have</u> to face those kids in Babylon. We have to learn the truth. And I know she's right. Besides, I owe her for putting her life on the line for me.

It's strange to think that tonight might be my last night on earth, that I may not live to see another sunset. But I've felt that way a hundred times in the past few months. For some reason, though, the possibility seems more real than it ever has.

I wonder what I'll dream.

THIRTEEN

One more beautiful day gone by, Sarah thought dismally. She gazed blankly out the window at the enormous fire on the lawn, where Caleb was brewing another stinking pot of the miraculous antidote for an ever-expanding mob of kids. *Another day where everyone is happy to be alive . . . except me.*

She tried to swallow around the lump in her throat. She couldn't cry anymore. Her tear ducts had been wrung dry. But when she saw that blissful smile on Caleb's face, she had only one thought.

That smile cost my brother his life.

It was true. Josh wouldn't have wanted her to look at the situation in such a cruel way, but she couldn't help it. Rage simmered inside her. He had given his life so that others could survive. He must have known the risks of broadcasting the antidote to the world. Oh, yes. He knew what the servants of the Demon could do; he'd exposed them.

In fact, he'd done far more than that. He'd *defeated* them. Now there was a cure for the plague. Now the Demon's greatest weapon was impotent, useless. The survivors would multiply bit by bit, and

123

the truth would spread . . . and those black-robed girls would be hunted down and eliminated—*annihilated* like the parasites they were.

And it was all because of her brother.

Sarah clenched her fists at her sides. How could *she* be the Chosen One? She was nothing compared to Josh. Absolutely nothing. *He* was the real hero, the real savior.

It was such a waste. But she wasn't only enraged at the *loss*. No, she was also enraged at herself. She never once told him what she truly thought of him, her innermost feelings . . . how much she loved his sense of humor, how much she admired his conviction and intellect. Of course not. She'd only pushed him around and made fun of him. She'd criticized him all the time. She'd even called him a *wimp*. A wimp! The person who'd sacrificed himself for everybody else's sake!

So stupid. So stupid. She squeezed her eyes shut. She had to redeem herself. She had to make sure that his memory lived forever, that every single survivor knew exactly what he had done, that they really and truly *understood* the appalling tragedy of his death—

"Sarah? Are you okay?"

She opened her eyes. Trevor stood right beside her. She hadn't even heard him come into the room. He reached out and touched her arm, eyeing her worriedly.

"Do you want to sit down?" he asked. He gently steered her back toward her desk, where the scroll lay waiting for her. "Here. Just take it easy for a while."

But all I've been doing is taking it easy, she thought in disgust.

She slumped down in the seat and groaned. Every day she sat in this room and reread the prophecies. Every day she promised herself she'd stop obsessing about Josh. But she might as well have stared at a brick wall. She'd accomplished nothing; she'd absorbed nothing. And invariably she found herself wandering over to the window and glaring down at the jubilant scene below, angrier and angrier. . . .

"I know it's hard," Trevor whispered.

Sarah shook her head. "I almost wish I hadn't even talked to him," she found herself confessing. "It's like . . . he died all over again." Her voice broke. She rubbed her eyes. "I thought he was dead nine months ago. I already came to terms with it. I didn't *need* this. . . ."

Trevor hugged her against him for a moment. She buried her face in his side and wept.

But it was amazing how good it felt . . . how the simple act of touching another human being alleviated some of the gnawing pain.

Thank you, Trevor.

Judging from the way he kept clinging to her, he was in as much need of an embrace as she was. And she was glad. Even though she'd only known him a month, she'd noticed a change in him. He seemed more *human* somehow. His voice was different. He no longer spoke in a flat monotone, as if he were simply processing information. It was as if he'd really started *feeling* things—emotions he'd kept buried deep inside him for years and years.

Finally he stood apart from her and took a deep breath.

"I guess you just have to think about the positive side of it," he murmured. "Josh saved so many lives with that one message. He really changed history, you know?"

She nodded. But she couldn't speak. Her throat was too tight.

Trevor lowered his eyes. "You also had a chance to speak to him one last time," he pointed out softly. "Hold on to that. You connected. And that's very lucky. I don't . . ." His voice trailed off. "I don't know if I'll ever have that chance."

"What do you mean?" she managed.

He shook his head and glanced out the window. "Ariel's never coming back. And the thing is, when I saw you talking to your brother . . . I don't know. It stuck with me." He swallowed. His lips were trembling. "I wish I could just say something to Ariel, you know, that I'm sorry about everything that happened—"

"You'll get your chance," Sarah interrupted. "I promise. Ariel will come back here. People are starting to hear about the cure." She hesitated. "And besides, I'm going to start spreading the word about Jezebel. I'm going to stop moping around and get off my butt. I'm going to tell everyone how she tricked people into believing that your sister was the Demon. Starting *now.*"

Trevor sighed deeply. "Speaking of Jezebel, have you noticed anything?"

Sarah raised her eyebrows. "What do you mean?"

126

"She hasn't shown her face around here in a really long time." He chewed on his lip. "She pretty much disappeared."

Sarah blinked a few times. Trevor was absolutely right. She'd been so wrapped up in her own grief that she hadn't even noticed. But the last time she'd seen Jezebel was over ten days ago—before she spoke to Josh, even.

"That wasn't in the scroll, was it?" Trevor asked. His voice was grave. "Her leaving, I mean?"

"No, it—it wasn't," she stammered. She glanced down at the parchment. "It says she's supposed to steal something from me—the 'key to the Future Time.'"

Trevor shrugged. "Maybe she already stole it."

Sarah stared back at him. Her thoughts started whirling. Was that possible? But *how?* She wasn't missing anything. The scroll was right in front of her, and her backpack was in the corner. Everything she owned was in that bag: her clothes, her journal; she'd opened it up this very morning. Nothing was gone.

"I don't think so," she muttered. "All my stuff is in this room."

"Well, maybe the key to the Future Time isn't like a *thing*—like a three-dimensional object," Trevor suggested. He folded his arms across his chest and leaned against the windowsill. "Maybe it's more of an *idea*. I was thinking . . . you know how you're always writing in your notebook? Maybe Jezebel went through your stuff and found some important piece of information in there. Maybe that's the key."

127

Goose bumps rose on Sarah's flesh. *Ugh.*

She didn't know if she agreed with him, but Jezebel probably *had* read her journal. After all, Sarah had spent most of her time trying to hide—to get a moment alone with the scroll. Her other possessions had always been wide-open and vulnerable. The more she thought about it, the more it made sense. *Damn.* She felt violated, as if somebody had just broken into her house. But there wasn't anything of value in her journal, was there? Not really. Just her thoughts and feelings and theories . . . and, of course, a complete translation of the Prophecies.

Unless . . .

"The code," she whispered.

Trevor nodded. "Exactly."

Oh, God. Her stomach dropped. If Jezebel had found the Prophecies and cracked the code, then . . . well, Sarah didn't even know what would happen. She couldn't even *guess.* It was a mystery, an *X* at the end of some unanswerable equation.

And that was infinitely more terrifying than any threat she could pin down.

"Anyway, that's part of the reason why I came up here to talk to you," Trevor mumbled. "I figure we better get moving on that code. And maybe I can help." He looked at her, then looked away. "I mean, I'm pretty good at math and stuff."

Sarah forced herself to nod. "Yeah, I *need* help. I need all the help you can give me."

Trevor offered a grim smile, then began pacing around the room. "Actually, I was thinking about

128

something today that might help. Have you ever heard of the Bible Code?"

Sarah's heart stirred painfully. The last time she'd ever talked to Josh in person, they'd *argued* about the Bible Code. "Yeah," she managed.

"What do you know about it?"

"Not much. My granduncle believed in it. He said that all of history was somehow encoded in the Torah. . . ." She hesitated. She'd always scoffed at the idea, shrugging it off as the ludicrous superstition of a clueless old man. But that was in a different time, in another world—a world without Visionaries or prophecies that came true.

"I used to think it was crap myself," Trevor mumbled. "But the math is kind of cool. I learned about it in a statistics class last year. The basic theory is that messages are hidden in the text of the Bible—the *original* text, in Hebrew. That's why I thought of it because your scroll is written in Hebrew, too. Anyway, the messages are supposedly hidden in equidistant letter sequences. But the thing—"

"I'm sorry," Sarah interrupted. "Hidden in *what?*"

Trevor paused by the door and smiled apologetically. "I'm sorry. Equidistant letter sequences. It works like this. You take a sentence and mush it all together so that there are no breaks between words. Now you have a long string of letters, right? Take the first letter of that string—then skip, say, five letters—then another five, and another five . . . and *those* letters spell out a message."

Wow. Sarah nodded slowly, her eyebrows tightly knit. That *did* sound pretty cool—at least, if she understood him correctly. Math hadn't been her strongest subject. Not by a long shot. Just hearing words like *equidistant* made her feel intimidated.

"So what you're saying is . . ." She didn't finish.

A shadow had appeared behind Trevor in the hall. Somebody was out there.

"Hey, guys."

Sarah's heart lurched. *No!*

"Jezebel?" Trevor cried, whirling around.

"No, you *idiot.*"

But it was Jezebel, all right. She brushed past Trevor in all her glory: black lipstick, black mascara, and a black dress that stood out like a raven's feathers against her pale skin. "How many times do I have to tell you people that I'm *not* Jezebel?"

Sarah remained frozen in her chair.

And that's when she saw it: a small pistol, clutched in Jezebel's right hand. It was the same shiny silver color as the rings on her fingers.

Oh, God. Don't do anything stupid. Please, Jezebel . . .

"I'm *not* Jezebel," she repeated, as if Sarah had spoken out loud. She flashed an empty smile. Her dark eyes glittered. "I thought you all knew that."

"You're Lilith," Trevor whispered. "You're the Demon—"

"Shut up, Trev." She groaned. "I'm not in the mood."

His face twisted in fury. All at once he lunged at her.

"Trevor, don't!" Sarah shrieked.

But the warning came too late. Jezebel jumped out of the way, twirled, then swatted Trevor on the back of the head with the butt of her gun.

"Ow!" he yelped. He stumbled and spun around. "What the . . ." He bristled, his eyes zeroing in on the gun.

"That's right." Jezebel chuckled and thrust the barrel at him, aiming it directly at the center of his chest. "Recognize this? It's one of yours."

"Jezebel, please," Sarah whispered. Her voice quivered—she couldn't stop it. "Don't hurt Trevor. Just tell me what you want, okay?"

Trevor's knees were visibly shaking. His skin had turned a sickly green.

"For starters, you can roll up the scroll on the desk," Jezebel commanded.

Sarah held up her hands. "Okay," she whispered. "Okay." She seized the wooden pegs and frantically twisted them, wrapping the parchment so tightly that it creaked. "Just stop pointing the gun at Trevor, all right?"

Jezebel laughed again. "But *why?* It's so much fun."

"Come on, Jez," Trevor croaked. His eyes flashed briefly to Sarah. "You don't want to do this. Let's just talk, okay?"

"What's there to talk about?" Jezebel murmured, blinking coquettishly.

Easy now. Sarah's grip remained tight on the scroll's handles. It felt nice and heavy in her hands. It would make a pretty good club, actually. But Jezebel was standing about five feet away—and Sarah was still sitting. By the time she got to her feet, Jezebel would have already had a chance to squeeze the trigger.

"You really want me to stop pointing the gun at you?" Jezebel asked.

Trevor nodded.

"Fine—"

Boom! An explosion blasted Sarah's eardrums, and Trevor was lifted off his feet. It was as if a pair of invisible hands had picked him up and tossed him across the room.

Sarah gaped in disbelief, ears ringing, as he collapsed in the corner. The tart smell of gunpowder hung in the air.

"Is that better?" Jezebel asked.

Sarah could hardly hear her. She was deaf, numb.

This isn't real. This is a nightmare.

Trevor's eyes were open, frozen in an expression of mild surprise. A small red spot appeared on his white T-shirt.

"Thank you very much," Jezebel said politely. She snatched the scroll off the desk. "I'll be taking that."

Don't. Stop . . .

A voice buried deep inside Sarah screamed at her to protest, to get up, to stop the murderer who was making off with the scroll. But she couldn't obey.

She could only watch, petrified, as Jezebel vanished out the door and into the fading afternoon sun.

COUNTDOWN
to the
MILLENNIUM
Sweepstakes

$2,000 for the year 2000

5...4...3...2...1 MILLENNIUM MADNESS.
The clock is ticking ... enter now to
win the prize of the millennium!

1 GRAND PRIZE:
$2,000 for the year 2000!

2 SECOND PRIZES: $500

3 THIRD PRIZES: balloons, noisemakers,
and other party items (retail value $50)

Official Rules
COUNTDOWN
Consumer Sweepstakes

1. No purchase necessary. Enter by mailing the completed Official Entry Form or print out the official entry form from www.SimonSays.com/countdown or write your name, telephone number, address, and the name of the sweepstakes on a 3" x 5" card and mail it to: Simon & Schuster Children's Publishing Division, Marketing Department, Countdown Sweepstakes, 1230 Avenue of the Americas, New York, New York 10020. One entry per person. Sweepstakes begins November 9, 1998. Entries must be received by December 31, 1999. Not responsible for postage due, late, lost, stolen, damaged, incomplete, not delivered, mutilated, illegible, or misdirected entries, or for typographical errors in the entry form or rules. Entries are void if they are in whole or in part illegible, incomplete, or damaged. Enter as often as you wish, but each entry must be mailed separately.

2. All entries become the property of Simon & Schuster and will not be returned.

3. Winners will be selected at random from all eligible entries received in a drawing to be held on or about January 15, 2000. Winner will be notified by mail. Odds of winning depend on the number of eligible entries received.

4. One Grand Prize: $2,000 U.S. Two Second Prizes: $500 U.S. Three Third Prizes: balloons, noise makers, and other party items (approximate retail value $50 U.S.).

5. Sweepstakes is open to legal residents of U.S. and Canada (excluding Quebec). Winner must be 20 years old or younger as of December 31, 1999. Employees and immediate family

members of employees of Simon & Schuster, its parent, subsidiaries, divisions, and related companies and their respective agencies and agents are ineligible. Prizes will be awarded to the winner's parent or legal guardian if under 18.

6. One prize per person or household. Prizes are not transferable and may not be substituted except by sponsors, in event of prize unavailability, in which case a prize of equal or greater value will be awarded. All prizes will be awarded.

7. All expenses on receipt and use of prize, including federal, state, and local taxes, are the sole responsibility of the winners. Winners may be required to execute and return an Affidavit of Eligibility and Release and all other legal documents that the sweepstakes sponsor may require within 15 days of attempted notification or an alternate winner will be selected.

8. By accepting a prize, a winner grants to Simon & Schuster the right to use his/her name and likeness for any advertising, promotional, trade, or any other purpose without further compensation or permission, except where prohibited by law.

9. If the winner is a Canadian resident, then he/she will be required to answer a time-limited arithmetical skill-testing question administered by mail.

10. Simon & Schuster shall have no liability for any injury, loss, or damage of any kind, arising out of participation in this sweepstakes or the acceptance or use of a prize.

11. The winner's first name and home state or province will be posted on www.SimonSaysKids.com or the names of the winners may be obtained by sending a separate, stamped, self-addressed envelope to: Winner's List "Countdown Sweepstakes", Simon & Schuster Children's Marketing Department, 1230 Avenue of the Americas, New York, NY 10020.

Sarah.   Josh.

   Ariel.   Brian.

     Harold.   Julia.

        George.

Don't grow too attached to them.
They won't live long.

Printed in the United States
By Bookmasters